The Inflatable Shop

Samuel Swain, captain, paced the floor of his shop. "Right then, shipmates," he said at last. "Things ain't as black as they was a while back. We have a captain and a plan of action now as proposed by the lad here. Namely, to get a message to the landlubbers below as 'ow we're in difficulties an' in need of help."

Henry nodded glumly. "Except that it's too late for that now," he said, and pointed towards the window. "We've left the beach behind. We're out at sea!"

Captain Swain and the others rushed out onto the veranda. A solitary seagull hovering at eye-level stared at them sadly, then, with a melancholy squawk, turned and wheeled dizzily downwards and away.

Captain Swain rubbed his chin. "Well then, shipmates," he said finally. "Which one of you has got a pen and which one of you can write a fairish hand, eh?"

Also available in Fontana Young Lions

A Bear Called Paddington – *Michael Bond*
Flossie Teacake's Fur Coat – *Hunter Davies*
Mists and Magic – *ed. Dorothy Edwards*
The Lily Pickle Band Book – *Gwen Grant*
The Last Vampire – *Willis Hall*
The Return of the *Antelope* – *Willis Hall*
Here Comes Charlie Moon – *Shirley Hughes*
My Best Fiend – *Sheila Lavelle*
Mind Your Own Business – *Michael Rosen*
Murdo – *Margot Speight*
The Boy Who Sprouted Antlers – *John Yeoman and Quentin Blake*

The Inflatable Shop

WILLIS HALL

Illustrated by

Babette Cole

Fontana Young Lions

First published in Great Britain 1984
by The Bodley Head Ltd
First published in Fontana Young Lions 1986
8 Grafton Street, London W1X 3LA

Fontana Young Lions is an imprint of
Fontana Paperbacks, a division of
the Collins Publishing Group

Printed in Great Britain by
William Collins Sons & Co. Ltd, Glasgow

1

Emily Hollins was hacking away with the kitchen scissors around the top of the breakfast-cereal packet. A dozen or so golden crunchy cornflake clusters tumbled out of the box and fell onto the kitchen floor.

"Oh, crikey!" murmured Emily's husband, Albert, surveying the mess.

"Never mind," said Emily, "I'll soon sweep it up. No use crying over spilt milk."

"It isn't milk," Albert pointed out. "It's Wheatie-Snax and they're honey-coated—they'll stick to everything. Right, Henry?"

Henry Hollins, their eleven-year-old son, glanced up from his book, *1001 Facts A Bright Boy Should Know*, vaguely waved his toast and marmalade, and nodded.

"Dare one ask, Emily," said Mr Hollins, "why you wanted to go cutting up that box in the first place?"

"Because," said Emily, triumphantly waving the packet-top in the air, "I needed this for the competition."

"I might have guessed it," grumbled Albert. "Another blinking competition!"

Emily Hollins was forever entering competitions. *Any* kind

of competition: crossword-puzzles; putting little crosses on football pictures in newspapers; guessing how many balloons could be jammed into one saloon-car at the local fête; spotting the differences between two pictures in a magazine. You name the competition, and Emily Hollins had gone in for it.

"What's this one about?" asked Albert, wearily.

"First of all," said Emily, "you have to collect the tops from six Wheatie-Snax packets."

Albert rather wished he hadn't asked.

"And then," Mrs Hollins went on, "you have to say which three countries these scenes on the back of the packet come from. If you get them right, the first prize is a world cruise."

"Oh, yes?" said Albert.

Albert studied the Wheatie-Snax packet at arm's length and screwed up his eyes. "It's dead simple," he said at last. "The first one is the Leaning Tower of Pisa—and that's in Pisa."

"Italy," said Henry, without looking up.

"And what about the Niagara Falls?" asked Albert.

"Ontario, Canada," said Henry.

"And how about the Sphinx? Whereabouts would you place that in its geographical context, at a rough guess?"

"Egypt."

"Good lad! Well done!" said Mr Hollins. "That wasn't too difficult at all, was it? World cruise here we come—"

"It's not *quite* that simple," said Emily.

"Ah," said Mr Hollins, "I thought there might be a catch in it."

"I've also got to think up a slogan saying why I like Wheatie-Snax."

"Go on then."

"How about," began Emily, frowning, "*I like Wheatie-Snax because they taste nice*?"

"I think we can forget about that cruise, Dad," said Henry.

"Yes," said his father. "Never mind though, we *are* off on holiday next week—even if we do have to pay for it ourselves."

"Not around the world though," said Emily, sadly.

"No, not quite," said Albert. "But Cockleton-on-Sea will make quite a nice change, if the weather's on our side."

"Do you want to know something?" asked Albert Hollins. "I don't think it's stopped raining *once* since the day we got here."

Emily Hollins looked up from the magazine she was reading. "Do you feel like passing the time by having a go at this competition with me?"

"No, thanks," sniffed Albert.

"How about you, Henry?"

Henry carefully marked his place in *The Book of Unusual Items*. Then he put the book down on the hard wooden bench in the paint-peeling sea-front shelter, looked up at his mother and shrugged. "What do you have to do?" he asked.

"First of all, you have to see how many words of three letters or more you can make out of the letters in *Chokko-Delight*. And then you have to think of a slogan of not more than twenty-five words beginning: *I like Chokko-Delight because* . . . Do you fancy having a try?"

"Not much," said Henry.

Emily pulled a face. "You'll both be green with envy," she said, "after I've won a luxury-caravan, or a fibre-glass motor-launch, or even a dream-home of my own choice."

"We'll just have to risk that," said Albert.

A silence followed, during which Emily's head was bent over her magazine while Albert and Henry sat gazing, bleakly, along the rain-drenched sea-front.

Gusts of rain swept across the golden domes and minarets of the South Pier, across the brown, sodden sand on the beach, and battered at the scrubbed decks and wheelhouse roofs of the fishing boats bobbing at anchor in the harbour. It almost obscured the red roof-tiles of the gaily coloured private hotels along the promenade, overlooking the sea: the Buona Vista, the St Claire, the Fredna, the Albemarle, Clovellies, the New Waterloo, and, away in the distance, the hotel where the Hollins family was staying, the Sea View.

Henry and Albert listened glumly as the raindrops drummed out their ceaseless tattoo on the cracked glass roof of the shelter where the three of them were sitting.

"How does this sound?" said Emily, at last. "*I like Chokko-Delight because of its delicious mouth-watering flavour, its scrumptious juicy raisins, and also because of its yummy-yum peanuts which I love to crunch between my teeth.*"

"Hey!" said Albert, impressed. "That's not half bad!"

"Except that that's thirty words," said Henry. "Five words too many."

"Oh, dear," said Emily.

"Another pipe-dream gone up in smoke," said Albert. He got to his feet and shook out the umbrella. "Come on," he said. "Let's go see what they've got to offer for lunch at Sea View."

Then, under the open umbrella, the three of them stepped

out of the shelter and set off along the promenade.

They walked past the deserted ice-cream stalls and putting green, past the grand entrance to the South Pier with its colourful posters announcing a WONDERFUL STAR-STUDDED ENTERTAINMENT twice-nightly at the end-of-the-pier theatre provided by a WHOLE HOST OF WORLD-FAMOUS ENTERTAINERS, and past the abandoned seaside-rock stall.

Beyond the seaside-rock stall was the sopping wet comic-postcard stand. And beyond the postcard stand was the locked and shuttered photographer's cabin. And beyond the photographer's cabin was the Inflatable Shop.

Henry's spirits rose slightly as he drew close to the Inflatable Shop. After three drenching days in Cockleton-on-Sea, Henry Hollins had decided that his favourite place was the Inflatable Shop. It was little more than a hut, but Henry called it the Inflatable Shop, simply because it sold inflatable goods.

All of the articles sold at the shop were on display outside the premises: bobbing balloons in all kinds of colours; inflatable plastic lifebelts in all shapes and sizes; multi-hued inflatable beach-balls; inflatable swimming-rings fashioned like swans; small inflatable arm-bands; large inflatable air-beds; all manner of inflatable craft from one-child canoes to adult-size dinghies; bright red inflatable toy-speedboats and huge unsinkable green tortoises.

All of these wonderful, curious articles had been blown up and lashed to the wooden railings, four walls and roof of the Inflatable Shop where, at this moment, they bounced and bobbed and tugged and pulled and squealed at their moorings in the same strong wind that was driving the rain along the promenade.

And it was not the goods alone that fascinated Henry—it was also the name of the shop's owner, Samuel Swain. It was painted over the open shop window in big, bold flowing gold letters, with lots of squiggles and swirls: SAMUEL SWAIN (PROP.) it said.

Peering out from underneath the umbrella, Henry spotted Samuel Swain standing in his usual place, just inside the doorway of the Inflatable Shop.

Samuel Swain had a wrinkled sun-bronzed round red face and he was as chubby as one of his own inflatable toy ducks. Henry guessed that Samuel Swain must have been a fisherman once, for he always dressed in fisherman's clothes: a roll-neck navy blue thick-knit jersey, thigh-length rubber boots doubled over at the knees and worn over navy blue heavy serge fisherman's trousers, and a navy blue cap with a black shiny peak. And he wore one gold ear-ring in his right ear.

"Come along, Henry—don't dawdle!" said Emily Hollins. "We don't want to be late for lunch."

Albert Hollins had also quickened his step. "We certainly don't," he said. "I've got a feeling that it's going to be prawn cocktails for starters!"

"It might be, easily," averred Emily, "if it isn't Brown Windsor soup."

They had now drawn level with the Inflatable Shop and, to Henry's surprise and pleasure, Samuel Swain waved across at them and called out cheerily, "Lovely weather for ducks!"

Albert Hollins blinked and cast a sidelong glance at the total stranger who had spoken to him. He muttered to Emily, under his breath: "It might suit the ducks, this weather—but it's not much use to me."

As they walked on past the Inflatable Shop, Mr and Mrs Hollins kept their eyes fixed firmly ahead. Henry tried to glance back but his mother grasped his hand. "Do *hurry*, Henry," she said.

Albert Hollins shifted his grip on the handle and lowered the umbrella slightly, head on into the teeth of the storm. Then, lengthening his stride even more, he led his family into the rain and wind with all the determination and purpose, Henry thought, of a Roman legionary marching bravely, shield upraised, into a shower of spears.

They were not late for lunch at the Sea View. As Albert, Emily and Henry entered the porch, the other guests were just filing into the dining-room.

Henry washed his hands, tugged a comb through his hair and joined his parents at the table. His father had been wrong about the lunch-starters. It wasn't prawn cocktails. It wasn't Brown Windsor soup either.

"Grapefruit segments again!" grumbled Albert. "We've only been here three days and this is the second time we've kicked off with grapefruit segments."

"Shush, dear," whispered Emily. "Don't fuss!"

Henry didn't particularly care for grapefruit segments either. What's more, he didn't particularly much care for liver-and-bacon. The liver-and-bacon arrived after the grapefruit segments. And the mashed potatoes which accompanied the liver-and-bacon were decidedly lumpy. Henry hated lumpy mashed potatoes. He put down his knife and fork and stared, despondently, at the rain beating down on the wilting geraniums in the hotel's window-boxes.

Albert and Emily didn't seem to mind the lumpy potatoes. They tucked into their meal energetically. So did the rest of the hotel's guests. The only sound to be heard was the chink-chunk of cutlery on plates.

"Do you suppose," began Henry, for the sake of saying something, "that his face is so red because he spends a lot of time blowing things up?"

"Who?" said Albert and Emily, in unison.

"Samuel Swain," said Henry. "The fat man in the fisherman's clothes, with the shop just past the pier."

"Oh, him," said Albert, pondering on the question then shaking his head, firmly. "No, I shouldn't think he blows up anything himself anyway—I should think he's probably got a machine for doing that. He won't do it by hand."

"Don't you mean, by mouth?" asked Emily.

Albert frowned at his wife, and then continued, "Mind you, come to think of it, he'll need *two* machines, won't he?"

"Why's that?" said Henry.

Albert Hollins chewed on a piece of rubbery liver, thoughtfully, and then said: "Well—he'll want one to put the gas in the balloons, right? So they sit up in the air on the end of their bit of string. But he won't put gas in the rubber boats and air-beds, will he?"

"Won't he?" asked Emily.

" 'Course not! If they were full of gas they'd be lighter than air—they'd float up off the sand and sail away into the clouds!"

"Well, I never!" said Emily.

"So what he'll have, I should imagine, is a cylinder of gas for his balloons and such—and then an air-pump for his dinghies and air-beds and so on. I expect he's got a red face from having spent a great deal of time in the open air. Does that answer your question?"

Henry nodded.

"Good," said his father. "Now finish your lunch before it gets cold."

Henry pushed his plate away. "I've finished now," he said.

"Well, then, Henry," said Emily, "put your knife and fork straight and just sit quietly until your father and me have finished ours."

Henry did as he was told. He gazed around the dining-room, restlessly. Wherever he looked he could see grown-ups forking lumpy potatoes into their mouths, as if they were heartily enjoying them.

There were no other children staying at the hotel. He knew that the couple at the window-table were called Mr and Mrs Midgeley, because he'd seen it on their suitcases when they arrived. He also knew that the two ladies at the table by the door, one tall-and-thin and the other not-so-tall-and-thin, and who dressed exactly alike down to their rimless spectacles and black jet beads, were sisters, and that their name was Pryce.

Henry blew out his cheeks and sighed. It was not, he decided, the most promising of beginnings to a holiday. If it went on like this, he'd have finished reading all the books he'd brought with him and he would have to look for a bookshop before the week was out.

2

"This is the life!" Albert murmured, happily, stretching back in his deck-chair, folding his arms behind his head, wiggling his bare toes and closing his eyes against the sun's glare.

Emily nodded. She took up her ballpoint pen and prepared to put the finishing touches to a newspaper competition in which she had just listed six kinds of biscuits in her order of preference and had only to compose a slogan of not more than eighteen words in length.

"*I like Granville's Tea-Time Assorted because* . . ." she wrote, and then paused to give the matter her utmost thought. "Let me see . . ." she said to herself and then she too closed her eyes and relaxed.

The sun had chosen to show itself before they had finished lunch. It had peered out from behind a huge grey cloud just after the Hollins family had finished the liver-and-bacon and just before the red-haired waitress with the hole in her stocking had served the dessert of tinned-peaches-and-strawberry-ice-cream.

Now, the sun was blazing down on the swarms of brightly dressed holiday-makers jostling along the pier or strolling past the busy putting green and seaside-rock stall with impatient children tugging at grown-ups' hands.

It was blazing down, too, on the countless boats, balloons and toys that were fastened to the walls and roof and veranda of the Inflatable Shop.

Henry had left his parents to sun themselves, put his *Thomms' Compendium of Interesting Oddities* in his pocket, just in case, and set off for a walk along the promenade. He had walked the full sun-baked length of it when he reached the Inflatable Shop. He paused a moment before stepping, with a slight flutter of excitement, across the threshold and into the shadowy, mysterious interior.

Strangely, there were no other customers inside the wooden building. Two women were standing outside on the veranda, looking at the articles on display. But apart from Samuel Swain and himself, the shop was empty.

"Arternoon, young 'un!" said Samuel Swain, with a broad wink. The old sailor bent his head as he removed a tube from the valve of the two-man speedboat he had just inflated. A beam of sunlight twinkled on his gold ear-ring. He looked up again. "Somethin' you was wantin' partickerly—or are you just window-shopping, cully?"

"Just window-shopping—I think," said Henry.

"You go ahead," said Samuel Swain, rising to his feet and lifting up the speedboat. "I'll just take this outside and lash it to the railings. I 'ad to let everythin' down and then give 'em all a blow-up agin after that storm—just to make certain that nothing had sprung a leak, like." Then, whistling a jaunty sea-shanty to himself, Samuel Swain stepped out onto the veranda with the inflated boat.

Henry, alone in the shop, stepped carefully around the metal cylinder, with its coiled rubber tubes, that the shop-owner had used to inflate the speedboat.

"Dad was right," said Henry to himself as he moved past a second set of inflating equipment. "There *are* two blowing-up machines—one must be air and the other one gas."

Without stopping by the central counter where most of the smaller goods were on display, Henry went straight to the back of the shop where the larger dinghies were hanging. He would have dearly loved to own one, and be able to paddle himself along the sea-coast. But he knew, even without looking at the price-tags, that his pocket-money wouldn't run to such a purchase—even if he saved up for weeks and weeks *and* included his birthday money in the bank.

"Considerin' puttin' to sea in a craft of your own then, are ye, sonny?" The old sailor had re-entered, quietly, and continued now as though he could read Henry's mind. "Thinkin' about spreadin' your wings, mebbe?" There was a twinkle in his eye. "Testin' your sea-legs an' doin' a mite of inshore sailin' along the coast?"

"How did you know?" gasped Henry, nodding dumbly.

"I was the same meself at your age," said Samuel Swain, lowering himself, carefully, onto an upturned bucket. He dipped his hand into a box on the counter and lifted out a bright balloon. "Why, shipmate," he went on, "many and many's the hour I spent as a lad, just leanin' on the sea-rail down by the harbour, gazin' at them fishin' boats. I was that desperate at ownin' a craft o' my own."

"And how long was it before you got one?"

Samuel Swain paused, stretched the balloon several times, expertly, between fingers and thumb, and then released one end, smartly, so that it snapped back against his hand. He reached out and drew the nozzle of an inflating machine towards himself and then pushed it into the neck of the balloon.

"Long enough," he said at last, in answer to Henry's question. "And then not until I'd studied sea-goin' ways as a deckie-learner on a deep-sea-goin' trawler out of Hull."

"I can't see me ever getting a boat," said Henry despondently. "Even if I could afford it, they wouldn't let me buy one."

"Them bein' your ma and pa, I take it?"

Henry nodded.

"P'raps what you're needin' is what I 'ad to 'ave—a bit of experience in boats?"

"I suppose you're right," said Henry. "But how do I set about getting it?"

The old sailor shrugged. "There's ways an' ways," he said, mysteriously, and then broke off. "Now, that *is* strange," he went on, looking down at the balloon that he had just inflated and which was lying, listlessly, on the wooden floor. "I ain't never knowed one of 'em lie down before—they're supposed to bob about in the air on the end of their strings—as chirpy as a foc'sle full o' parrots!"

"You know what you've done wrong, don't you?" said Henry.

"Sink me, if I do!"

Henry couldn't help but smile. "You've used the wrong machine to blow it up," he said. "You've put air inside it instead of gas!"

"I'll be a sea-captain's uncle!" roared Samuel Swain. "I do believe you're right, young 'un!" And then he frowned and rubbed his stubbly chin. "Hang on a second though," he muttered. "I *can't* 'ave done—for I used that other one to blow up all them floatable goods I got lashed to the walls an' roof an' so on—an' that'd mean that . . ." His voice trailed away.

"What would it mean?" asked Henry.

"It don't 'ardly bear thinkin' of—but it'd mean that all o' them dinghies an' airbeds an' such that I've got blowed up out there was full o' gas instead o' air!"

"Would that be a problem?" asked Henry.

"A *problem*, me hearty, why—" Samuel Swain broke off.

At the same moment, Henry grabbed at the counter for support as the floor beneath him shook.

"Hold tight, lad!" ordered the old sailor. "There it goes again!"

The entire Inflatable Shop, it seemed, was shifting on its foundations. Henry did as he had been told and held on, tightly, and with both hands. In front of his eyes, a blue inflated plastic rabbit, clutching between its paws a vivid orange plastic carrot, teetered across the counter-top to the very edge, wobbled, leaned forward, and then toppled to the floor. At the back of the shop, the hanging plastic dinghies creaked, complainingly, and swung on their ropes.

"What's happening, Mr Swain?" gasped Henry.

The answer to his question came not from the old seafarer but from someone who had just entered and was standing by the door. "I hope you realize," the voice began, sharply, "that this *entire* establishment has left the ground completely and is floating some ten feet or so in the air?"

Henry turned and recognized the speaker instantly. It was the taller of the two Miss Pryce sisters who sat at the table near the door in the dining-room of the Sea View hotel. He recollected that, when he had entered the Inflatable Shop, there had been two women on the veranda. He guessed that the other one must have been the second of the Pryce sisters and wondered whether she was there still.

The taller of the sisters answered his unspoken question: "It really is quite unforgivable! I must insist that you return us to the ground at once! My sister is of an extremely nervous disposition! How do you think she must feel at finding herself suspended above the promenade in a sea-front novelty shop?"

"I'm quite all right, Augusta—don't fuss!" said the second Miss Pryce entering, a trifle breathlessly, from the veranda. She patted her back hair into place and fiddled with her beads. "It was just the initial shock of taking off that startled me—now that I'm actually up here I feel quite . . . calm."

"Nonsense, Mildred," snorted her sister. "All these years you have refused, point-blank, even to go up in an aeroplane! Why have we always spent our holidays at Cockleton-on-Sea? If you're going to tell me now that you don't mind being up in the air—why, we could have gone off, years ago, and enjoyed ourselves on the Costa-del-Sol or the Bay of Naples!"

"My dislike of flying wasn't the only reason we've never been abroad!" retorted the shorter of the two. "After all, we could have gone by boat. No, it was because you've always said that you didn't like foreign food."

"Did you know," interpolated Henry, "that Painted Lady

butterflies fly all the way from Africa, across the Mediterranean and Europe, to England each summer?"

The sister who wasn't Mildred ignored him. "Not *all* foreign food, I never said that!" she argued. "I'm quite fond of a *spaghetti bolognese* or a *paella* now and then."

While the Pryce sisters had been bickering, Samuel Swain had crossed to the door and now looked down. He beckoned to Henry to join him. "Swamp me," the old seadog muttered, "we have taken off all right!"

Henry and Samuel moved out onto the veranda. Henry leaned on the fencing and looked down.

If they had been two metres above the ground when the Misses Pryce had entered the shop, they must have been gaining height steadily ever since.

Far down below, Henry could see the South Pier, the promenade, the seaside-rock stall, the sea-front hotels and all of Cockleton-on-Sea spread out beneath, looking like the miniature village in the town's ornamental park.

"We're rising faster every second, sonny—but there's no call to alarm the women-folk," said Samuel Swain. "We'll soon have the situation ship-shape, ladies!" he called back into the shop. "But until we get things sorted out, it might be best if you both stayed inside!" He closed the door on them, softly.

Henry peered down over the veranda, and tried to spot his parents among the ant-sized sun-bathers on the beach.

He wondered what he should do if his parents were to glance up and see their son hovering in the wooden hut above their heads. Should he wave down to them? He had a feeling that neither his mother nor his father would appreciate the sight of

their only son taking to the air in a novelty-shop.

As it happened, none of the folk in Cockleton-on-Sea had noticed the Inflatable Shop leaving the ground. And now, the full glare of the sun beating down prevented them from seeing it hanging above their heads in the cloudless sky.

Henry held on tight to the veranda-rail, leaned over, and

looked down once again. "I think we've stopped rising, Mr Swain," he said.

"Lucky for us then, shipmate," said the sailor. "Let's hope our good fortune holds and we sets down again just where we put out from. For if we puts down on the pier or in the middle of the promenade, I'll be in terrible trouble with the Town Council."

"We seem to be holding height," said Henry. "I'm sure we're not going down—but it does seem as if we're *moving*—as if we're being carried by the wind across the beach."

The old sailor licked his forefinger and held it up. "You're right, young 'un," he said. "There's a breeze up here that ain't a-blowin' down below. An' if my calculations ain't wrong, it's carryin' us out to sea!"

Henry shaded his eyes and peered seawards. It was true. They were heading slowly but steadily towards the open sea. "Shall we try and shout down for help, Mr Swain?" he asked.

Samuel shook his head. "We're far too high for anyone down there to hear us. Might as well save our breath."

"Then what *can* we do?"

"I don't rightly know, not offhand," confessed the sailor. "But one thing's certain, shipmate—we'll 'ave to acquaint our female passengers with the serious nature of our circumstances."

"And not before time too!" said Augusta Pryce who, unnoticed, had opened the door of the shop and was standing, just behind them, on the veranda.

"After you, ma'am," said Samuel Swain, politely, inviting her back into the interior of the shop.

I like Granville's Tea-Time Assorted because they give you a better assortment than any other kind of biscuit. Emily Hollins counted up the words that she had written down, and sighed.

"Nineteen," murmured Emily to herself. "One word too many." Then, putting down pen and paper, she yawned, leaned back in her deck-chair and looked up into the sky—at the very same moment that the only patch of cotton-wool cloud in the vast expanse of blue chose to drift across the face of the sun. For a fleeting moment, Emily glimpsed a curious object high above and drifting out towards the horizon. She sat bolt upright, blinked and stared again. But the cloud had gone on its way and the sun dazzled her eyes.

"Albert!" she said, giving her husband a sharp dig with her elbow.

"Ouch!" Albert grumbled, waking at once. He rubbed his eyes and looked around. "Where's Henry?"

"I don't know—gone for a stroll along the sea-front."

"What did you wake me up for?"

"Because I saw something." She pointed into the sky. "Up there."

"I can't see anything," said Albert, screwing his eyes and staring into the sun's rays.

"It's gone now."

"What was it?"

"I don't know—something moving across the sky—high up."

"An aeroplane, I suppose."

"It wasn't *shaped* like an aeroplane," said Emily. "It was a sort of square-shape. Like a house."

Albert Hollins suppressed a giggle.

"Don't laugh," snapped Emily. "And it had *things* round the side—almost like balloons but not quite—and all different shapes."

"A square-shaped object with different things all round it. Very likely." Albert chuckled again and promptly closed his eyes.

Emily gave an irritated sigh and took up her pen and paper. "I like Granville's Tea-Time Assorted," she said to herself, "because . . ."

"Personally speaking, I fail to see what all the fuss is about," said Augusta Pryce, primly. "If all those things round the side are keeping us up because they're full of gas—surely, all you have to do is let the gas out gently and we'll float back down?"

Samuel Swain shook his head. "You see, ma'am, we're finely balanced on an even keel. If I was to go a-letting gas out of any o' those contraptions, who's to say as 'ow we wouldn't lose that balance, tip up, and all go tumbling over the side?"

"He's right, Augusta," said Mildred Pryce, fiddling nervously with her beads.

"Oh, do be quiet, Mildred," said Augusta, sharply. "What do you know about 'balance' anyway? You never even learned to ride a bicycle!"

Samuel Swain brought his fist down on the counter in an attempt to bring the meeting to order. "First things first, I allus say, an' argufyin' arterwards. And our first task now is to . . ." He broke off and scratched the stubble on his chin. "I'll be a monkey's uncle if I c'n remember now *what* our first task is!"

"Shouldn't our first task be to try and let someone on the ground know that we're up here?" suggested Henry.

"Blow me down," said Samuel Swain, "if the young 'un ain't gone and put 'is finger on the very nub of the situation! Well done, lad!"

"Thank you, Mr Swain."

"Exceptin', what you've put your finger on, son, is the *second* most important thing. It's come back to me now what I was goin' to say. Our first task, I reckons, is to appoint ourselves a captain."

"A *captain*!" snorted Augusta. "Whatever do we need a captain for?"

"Why, to put an end to all this squibblin' an' squabblin' for a start. We need somebody in charge. We don't know how long we're going to be up here—"

"Not until tea-time, I hope," put in Mildred. "Augusta and I have tickets for the Star-Studded Entertainment at the Pier Theatre—the curtain goes up at seven-thirty, and we—"

"I was about to say, ma'am," Samuel cut her short, "we none of us know how long we're going to be up here for, and I never did hear tell of a ship as didn't sail the better for havin' a skipper at the helm."

"I vote for Mr Swain for captain," said Henry.

"I never heard such nonsense!" said Augusta. "In the first place, this isn't a ship we're in, it's a novelty-shop—I never heard of a novelty-shop that needed a captain before!"

"I think the gentleman may be right, Augusta," said Mildred. "If we *are* going to get to the Pier Theatre this evening, we've got to trust someone to get us down from here."

"Supposin' we take a vote on it?" suggested Samuel Swain. "Hands up all them as wants me for skipper?"

The old sea-salt put his own hand up, and so did Henry and Mildred. The hands of Augusta Pryce, however, remained firmly by her side.

"Motion carried," said Samuel, "by three votes to one."

Augusta sniffed. "You may vote as much as you like," she said, "but I'm *certainly* not taking orders from you, my man."

"And why not, ma'am?"

"Because if you hadn't been so stupid as to put gas inside those inflatable things outside, we wouldn't be in this ridiculous predicament. And secondly," Augusta paused and then pointed a finger at her sister, "secondly, I would never ever vote for anything that silly little numbskull voted for!"

"Augusta!" gasped Mildred.

"I'm sorry, Mildred, but truth will out. You have never ever been right about *anything* in your entire life."

Mildred Pryce was very nearly in tears. "However can you say such things! I was right only yesterday, if you'd care to cast your mind back! Who was it that insisted we take the umbrella when we went out for our evening stroll? Never right indeed! If it had not been for me, you would have got positively *soaked*!"

"Ladies, ladies!" said Samuel, banging his hand on the counter yet again. "There'll be no more quarrelling aboard this craft! Now—I'm your duly appointed captain and my word is law!"

Samuel Swain, captain, pushed his cap to the back of his head and paced the floor of the shop. "Right then, shipmates," he said at last. "Things ain't as black as they was a while back, I think you must agree. We have a captain and a plan of action now as proposed by the lad here. Namely, to get a message to the landlubbers below as 'ow we're in difficulties an' in need of help." He beamed at Henry. "Wasn't that your plan?"

Henry nodded, glumly. "It was," he said, and pointed towards the window. "Except that it's too late for that now. We've left the beach behind. We're out at sea!"

Captain Swain and the Pryce sisters rushed out onto the veranda. Henry joined them.

A solitary seagull hovering at eye-level stared at them sadly, then, with a melancholy squawk, turned and wheeled dizzily downwards and away.

"I wonder how fast gulls fly?" mused Henry. "Someone once recorded a peregrine falcon flying at two hundred and seventeen miles per hour in a stoop for its prey."

They watched the gull till it was a white speck over the grey-green swell far below.

Captain Swain rubbed his chin. "Well then, shipmates," he said at last. "Which one of you has got a pen and which one of you can write a fairish hand, eh?"

3

Hugo McMurdo, the gnarled and bearded skipper of the fishing-boat, *Highland Lassie*, tugged at the cord that loosed his catch and a silvery, shining cascade of mackerel tumbled onto the deck, covering the old Scotsman's sea-boots until he stood ankle-deep in tail-slapping fish.

"Will ye look at that, mon!" crowed the sea-captain, gazing in delight at the size of his catch. "We've enough here tae ca' it a day!"

"Beg pardon, skipper?" said Frank Throstlethwaite, the ship's bosun and only other member of the crew, who was standing nearby.

"Awa', laddie, an' wash yer ears oot!" replied McMurdo, grumpily.

Many, many years had passed since Hugo McMurdo had moved down from the Scottish coast to fish the waters outside Cockleton-on-Sea, but he had never lost his Highland Scots accent. Throstlethwaite, who had sailed with the Scotsman for a number of those years, still had difficulty in understanding his skipper.

The two men worked in separate silence for several minutes, each deep in his own thoughts.

Throstlethwaite, on the deck of the fishing-boat, loaded the catch into large wicker baskets. "It's not much fun," he muttered to himself, "spending one's life at sea with a man who speaks a foreign language!"

McMurdo, his hands on the wheel, gloomily contemplated the heaving ocean through the wheelhouse window. "There's nae pleasure," he grumbled to himself, "in spendin' yer life afloat wi' a man who's as deaf as a dyin' haggis!"

Suddenly, the bosun called out to him, "Skipper! Look what I've found!" McMurdo leaned out of the wheelhouse. "What's tae do, mon?"

"It's a bottle, skipper!" called back the bosun, holding up the article in question that he had found in the catch.

"Whisht awa'—I can no tarry wi' bottles!" shouted McMurdo. "Heave it back into the sea, mon!"

"Beg pardon, skipper?"

"Throw it over the side, laddie!"

"But it's got a message in it!"

The wrinkled Scot's bushy white eyebrows shot up in surprise. "A message, d'y'say? Well, don't stand there ditherin' like a sassenach on Ben Nevis, bosun! Bring it here!"

The bosun made his way with his important find along the deck and into the wheelhouse.

"Open it, mon," said Hugo McMurdo, impatiently. "Seventy year I've sailed the seas, mon an' lad, but this is the first time it's happened tae me!"

McMurdo watched, eagerly, as Throstlethwaite unscrewed the cap of the bottle and took out the folded piece of paper that was inside.

The bosun cleared his throat, importantly, and studied the paper. "Why, captain!" he exclaimed. "It's dated the nineteenth of August—that's today! It could only have been in the water for a few hours at the very most!"

The old sea-captain sniffed, disappointed at this news. No treasure map, then, from some long-lost shipwrecked mariner on a palm-fringed desert island . . . "Just ma' luck!" thought Captain McMurdo, but he said aloud: "Go on then, mon—read it oot!"

"It's addressed to a Mr and Mrs A. Hollins, c/o The Sea View Private Hotel, The Promenade, Cockleton-on-Sea." The bosun broke off with a gasp of surprise. "Would you believe it!" he went on. "That's just around the corner from my Auntie Flo and Uncle Cedric's house! It just goes to show you, skipper, doesn't it?"

"Goes tae show ye what?"

"Why—what a small world it is really!"

"Get on with the message, ye stupid mon!"

"*Dear Mum and Dad*," read Bosun Throstlethwaite. "*This is to let you know that I am somewhere over the sea in Samuel Swain's shop. Miss Pryce and Miss Pryce are here as well. Can you send someone? Weather O.K. so far. Your loving son, Henry. P.S. Please excuse small writing.*"

"Is that all it says?" said the skipper.

The bosun nodded. "That's all," he said. "What do you make of it?"

"Hoots, mon—it's naught but a load o' blather! Stick it back in yon bottle and throw it back over the side!"

"But, skipper, it might be important—"

"Awa', laddie! It's a load o' hogwash! Gone tae sea in a shop? It does nae make sense, mon!"

"But, skipper—"

"Are ye going to obey ma' orders, bosun, and throw that rubbish back, or am I tae enter yer name in ma' log-book in red ink—and make ye suffer the attendant consequences?"

The bosun sighed and gave in. The last time that the skipper had written his name in the log-book in red ink, he had had to suffer the attendant consequence of scrubbing down the *Highland Lassie* from prow to stern, above and below decks.

He drew back his arm and threw, as far and as hard as he could. The bottle soared through the air in a wide arc and landed with an empty-sounding "plop" in the rising swell where it sank immediately and was lost for all time.

The bosun staggered slightly as he moved back across the deck. A blustery wind was getting up, causing the little fishing-boat to bob and sway on a pitching sea. A shower of spray rose over her bulwarks and lashed the wheelhouse window.

"Aye," muttered Hugo McMurdo to himself. "It's just as well we're heading back to harbour—there's a storm blowing up."

"But supposing nobody *finds* the bottle?" asked Henry, gripping the counter tightly as the shop swung in the wind.

"We can only hope against hope that they do, young 'un," said Samuel Swain.

"I've never heard of anything so ridiculous in my entire life," said Augusta Pryce. "That tiny insignificant bottle in that vast and lonely ocean! Why—there is not the remotest possible chance of anyone finding it!"

"But they *do* get found, Augusta," objected Mildred, making a quick grab at the corner of the store-cupboard in order to keep her balance, as the shop hit a minor air-pocket and dipped sharply at one corner, "I've often read about such things in stories."

"Stories!" scoffed Augusta. "If you spent more time studying real-life happenings and less time with your nose in story-books, you might have more sense to show for it!"

Instead of trying to argue with her sister, Mildred changed the subject. "I do feel hungry," she said in a small voice. "I'm sure it must be almost dinner-time. I do wish we were back at Sea View."

"We must put our minds to the predicament we're in at present, ma'am," said Captain Swain, firmly, "and stop wishing ourselves elsewhere." The Inflatable Shop was tossing and swaying more with every passing minute. "I fear there's a gale on the way, and we're ill-prepared for it."

"What do you want us to do, captain?" asked Henry.

"That's what I likes to hear," said Samuel, looking sternly at the Misses Pryce, "a member o' the crew as is ready to show a bit of willingness." He turned back to Henry. "Have you got the stomach for going outside with me in this weather?"

"I think so," said Henry, uncertainly.

"Right then. We ain't had a look at them inflatables out there since we took off. There's one or two of 'em may be needing a touch more gas."

"Hadn't we better make sure they're tied down tightly, too,

if there's bad weather on the way?" asked Henry. In for a penny, in for a pound, he decided.

"My thinking exactly. Good lad!"

"What about us?" said Mildred, feeling rather ashamed of herself for having complained.

"Seeing as 'ow you've asked, ma'am, an' seeing as 'ow it was you yourself complaining about the pangs of hunger—how about you takin' on the duties of ship's cook?"

"Her!" Augusta laughed out loud. "She couldn't boil an egg if you wrote down the instructions!"

"I don't mind having a *try*," Mildred said, doubtfully. "But what is there to cook?"

"We're not entirely without provisions," said Samuel. "I may not be prepared for every contingency in life—such as this shop taking to the air in the way it did. On the other hand, I'm not the sort o' sea-going chap as ain't ready for the odd rainy day that comes along." He pointed to the large store-cupboard. "Look in there."

Mildred opened the cupboard doors. The inside was a mass of drawers and shelves and cubby-holes.

"Look on the second shelf from the bottom," said Samuel.

Mildred knelt down. "There are tins of things!" she said, excitedly.

"That there are, ma'am," agreed Samuel. "Soups an' suchlike. One large Mulligatawny; one large Oxtail; one large Mixed Vegetable; one small Minestrone. I think you'll also find a family-sized Treacle Pudding and a tin o' custard to go with it. On top o' which, you'll find a tin-opener, a small paraffin-stove, and a box o' matches on the bottom shelf."

"We can have a veritable feast!" Mildred enthused. "Which soup would you like me to prepare?"

"None of 'em, ma'am," said Samuel, ruefully. "The tinned stuffs we'll put by for rationing. But if you'll glance again at the second shelf, you'll see a paper package standing next to the treacle pud."

"This one?"

"That's it, ma'am. It contains a few comestibles I prepared afore leavin' 'ome this morning—with the intention of consumin' 'em this afternoon on the sands. Only events overtook me, as you might say. There's four sardine-and-tomato sandwiches in brown bread, that's one each. There's also a fair-sized lump o' cheese an' a handful of biscuits. Lastly, there's a hard-boiled egg." Samuel paused, took off his cap and scratched his head. "Now, speaking frankly, I don't see as 'ow one hard-boiled egg can be decently split four ways? Do you, young 'un?"

Henry shook his head. "No, captain."

"So what do you say, lad, if we calls it a matter o' ladies first and allows them to share it atwixt the two of 'em?"

"Suits me," said Henry.

"Thank you, both of you," said Mildred, very touched by this unselfishness.

"I notice," began Augusta, who had remained visibly unimpressed by all that had been said, "that while you've told us what we're going to eat—you haven't mentioned drink?"

"I haven't, ma'am, no. I was leaving the bad news until last." Samuel Swain paused and clutched at a beam as the shop danced about in a fresh gust of wind. "We're not too well off in that direction, I'm afraid. There's a bottle o' cold tea on the third shelf down from the top, an' that's all we 'as to sustain ourselves."

"Cold tea!" Augusta shuddered.

"While I'm out on the veranda, it's my intention to rig up some sort o' device for catching rain-water—we shouldn't go short o' water at the very least."

"You haven't told me yet," said Augusta, "what my task is supposed to be?"

"Thank you for remindin' me, ma'am, but I ain't forgotten. Tell me now, have you 'ad any previous experience of map-readin' or chartin' a course by the stars?"

"Certainly," Augusta began. "When I was a girl I bicycled along the highways and byways of Great Britain—by map by day and by the heavens after nightfall."

"That's the best bit o' news so far!" cried the captain, delighted. "Well, ma'am, if you'd care to feel in that cubby-'ole on the third shelf down, you'll find a book o' maps an' charts an' such. P'raps you'd care to set about chartin' our exact geographical location?" He crossed to the door and pulled his cap down firmly on his head. "Come on, young 'un. Let's see what needs to be done outside."

He placed his shoulder to the door and pushed, hard. Because of the force of the wind, it took all his strength to open the door. Then he held open the door for Henry, who brought with him the long thin tube that led to the cylinder of inflating-gas.

Henry Hollins had to struggle hard to keep his balance on the veranda. The biting wind whistled and howled about his ears and threatened to whisk his legs from under him.

"You all right, young 'un?" Captain Swain had to shout at the top of his voice to make himself heard.

Henry nodded. Bracing themselves against the wind, they worked their way along the veranda. The captain pushed a testing thumb into an air-bed here, tightened a sheepshank or reef-knot there, and adjusted the pressure somewhere else. Henry stood at his side, ready to put a helping finger on a half-tied knot or nip the valve on an inflatable as Captain Swain increased or decreased the gas-pressure.

And, all the while, the howling wind attempted to blow them off the veranda and into the grey and pitching sea below.

Inside the Inflatable Shop, Augusta Pryce flicked through the pages of a *Junior School Atlas*. It was the only book she had been able to find in the store-cupboard. "You couldn't plot a course with this!" she announced, contemptuously, tossing the atlas aside. "It isn't any use at all."

Mildred looked up from the supper she was arranging neatly on the counter. "*You* couldn't plot a course with anything," she challenged her sister. "Why did you tell the captain all those lies about having cycled across Great Britain? You never bicycled any farther than the park down the road—and then only in broad daylight."

"I had no intention," said Augusta, "of revealing my ignorance in front of a common shop-keeper and a small rude boy."

"Don't you realize that they're both out there now, risking their lives for us?" countered Mildred. "*And* they've let us have the only egg," she added, divesting it of its shell.

"Indeed," snapped Augusta.

Mildred said nothing. She sliced the egg in two and checked the rest of the food laid out: four sardine-and-tomato sandwiches; four small portions of cheese and biscuits. It didn't seem very much.

Mildred sighed and her thoughts flew back to the comforts of Cockleton-on-Sea. "I wonder what they're having for dinner at the Sea View," she said, and added, wistfully: "I wish I were back there now."

The red-haired waitress with the hole in her stocking crossed the dining-room balancing three plates of soup in her hands. She arrived without accident at the Hollins' table and then frowned as she considered the members of the Hollins family sitting there. "Hey?" she said. "You are a three at this table, aren't you?"

"That's what we're beginning to wonder ourselves," sighed Emily. "We *were* a three at lunch-time—but we suddenly seem to have gone down to two. Our son, Henry, wandered off this afternoon and we can't imagine where he's got to."

"That's funny," said the red-haired waitress. "The two Miss Pryces have gone missing as well." She nodded across at the empty table by the door. "It's not like them to be late for a meal-time."

"How odd!" said Emily.

"Anyway, I'll leave you the three soups just in case," said the red-haired waitress. "You might as well have them—you'll have them to pay for whatever happens—" She broke off and clapped a hand to her mouth. "Trust me!" she said. "I'd forget my head if it wasn't screwed on!"

"Why?" said Albert Hollins. "What have you forgotten?"

"There's a gentleman waiting to see you in the hall."

Albert frowned. He didn't want his soup to get cold. "What kind of a gentleman?" he asked.

"Quite a smart gentleman. He's wearing a striped suit, a diamond-patterned pullover and a spotted tie."

"You'd better go and see who he is, Albert," said Emily. "It might be something to do with Henry."

"I suppose so." Mr Hollins put his paper napkin on the table, got up and left the dining-room.

Emily sank her spoon into her soup and peered at the competition in the evening edition of the *Cockleton-on-Sea Telegraph and Argus*.

"*Our artist*," she read, "*has made several deliberate mistakes in drawing the picture above. How many of them can you spot? Draw a ring round each mistake*."

Emily pursed her lips and studied the picture of a farmyard, carefully. "Well," she said, "a sheep hasn't got five legs for a start—"

"Excuse me," said a voice at her elbow, "but could I impose upon you for the pepper?"

It was Mr Midgeley, a fellow-guest, who was sitting at the next table with his wife, Mrs Midgeley. Mr Midgeley had a gold watch-chain across his waist-coat and Mrs Midgeley had had her hair done with a purplish blue rinse.

Emily smiled across at them. "Of course you can," she said, handing over the plastic pepper-pot.

"*Merci beaucoup!*" said Mr Midgeley.

"I hope you won't think we're nosey-parkering," said Mrs Midgeley, "but we couldn't help overhearing what you were saying about your little boy being missing."

"We'd just like to say," said Mr Midgeley, "that we hope everything turns out for the best."

"For the *very* best," echoed Mrs Midgeley.

"Thank you both, very much," said Emily, putting on a brave smile.

Out in the hall, the man in the striped suit, diamond-patterned pullover and spotted tie, held out his hand to Albert Hollins. "Mr Hollins, I presume?" he said.

"That's right," said Albert. "What can I do for you?"

"My name's Frank Throstlethwaite," said the man. "I'm the bosun on the *Highland Lassie*, a fishing-boat that sails from the harbour here."

"Oh, yes?" said Albert, coldly, thinking of his plate of soup and wishing that the man would come to the point.

"To cut a long story short," said Throstlethwaite, "we picked this up in one of our nets this afternoon—it was in a bottle." He handed a crumpled piece of paper to Albert who glanced at it as the bosun continued, "My skipper, Mr McMurdo, wanted me to sling it straight back in the sea. But I fooled him and threw the empty bottle back. I knew I would be in this vicinity tonight. I'd promised to pop round and see Auntie Flo and Uncle Cedric—they live just round the corner . . ." He broke off as he realized that Albert's attention was directed to the note. "Does it make any sense to you?" he asked. Albert Hollins scratched his head. "Well, yes and no," he said.

"Is it important?"

"It might be. It's from our son, Henry. I don't quite understand it, but I'm extremely grateful to you for bringing it round."

"Don't mention it. I came as quickly as I could. Well—as soon as I'd had a bath and put a suit on. My Auntie Flo's just

bought a new three-piece suite. She goes round the twist if I sit down on it in my fishing togs."

"You can't blame her," said Albert, smiling at the bosun. He was ashamed at himself for being a trifle short with his visitor earlier on. After all, the man had come here to do him a favour. "Have you had your dinner yet?" he asked.

"No—why?"

"I wonder if you'd care to have a bite with us?" Albert paused, and then added: "You'd be more than welcome. I know my wife will be keen to see this note. The thing is, we've got three dinners ordered and paid for anyway—and it doesn't look as if Henry will be back this evening . . . Why don't you?"

"I usually have a snack at Auntie's," said the bosun, doubtfully. "She does me a sandwich or some cheese-and-pickled-onions. What are you having here?"

"Brown Windsor soup for starters. I think the main course is Roast Lamb."

"Really?" The bosun's interest perked up. "It's not a hard-and-fast arrangement I have with Auntie Flo," he said. "Either I turn up or I don't. It's as simple as that."

"So there's no reason at all why you shouldn't stop and have some dinner with us?"

"None whatsoever."

Albert Hollins took the bosun's elbow and steered him towards the dining-room.

Mildred Pryce was beginning to wish that she hadn't eaten the sardine-and-tomato sandwich; or the cheese-and-biscuits; or even the half-a-hard-boiled-egg. She glanced around at her three companions who were clinging, as she was herself, to the stoutest beams in the Inflatable Shop.

The storm was at its very height. Heavy rain was rattling down on the corrugated-iron roof. The shop was being buffeted around the darkening sky like a matchbox in a mountain stream.

An inflated dinghy, which had been hanging up on display inside the shop, broke loose from its moorings and bounced around their heads like an enormous rubber-ball.

Samuel Swain, watching the wayward dinghy, was pleased that he and Henry had checked the ropes outside before the full force of the storm had hit them. He was reasonably sure that they would hold. But would the shop itself? The timber frame was creaking, and the boards groaning, complainingly. How much more of this kind of treatment could the wooden structure take? Not a lot, he reckoned. All the same, there was no sense in alarming the others.

"Hold on!" he called out. "The storm'll blow itself out soon!"

"You stupid man!" cried Augusta, half in anger and half in fear. "How do *you* know *what* the storm is going to do? Probably get worse I shouldn't wonder!"

"Oh, do be quiet, Augusta!" snapped Mildred. "Things are bad enough without your complaining!"

Henry Hollins clung firmly to the beam, too, and grinned to himself at this development in Mildred's character.

"Did you know," he said to nobody in particular, "that in Java there are thunderstorms on approximately three hundred and twenty-two days of the year?"

4

Bosun Throstlethwaite swallowed his last mouthful of orange jelly and ice-cream and licked the spoon.

"Thanks very much, Albert," he said, "for a smashing meal!"

"It's been a pleasure, Frank," said Mr Hollins.

The bosun got to his feet. "Time I was on my bike," he said.

"Wouldn't you like to stay for a cup of coffee, served in the TV lounge?" asked Albert.

"No, ta—I'd better push off," said the bosun, glancing at the clock on the mantelpiece. "If I leave now I'll still have time to drop in at Auntie Flo's—a piece of cheese and a few pickled onions would finish the evening off nicely. Thanks again, Albert. Ta-ta, Mrs Hollins."

"What a nice man," observed Emily, as the bosun set off towards the dining-room door.

Albert's mind was already on other matters. He pulled the crumpled note from Henry out of his pocket. "It was nice of him to bring this round too," he said. "But I still haven't worked out what it means, exactly."

"Never mind," said Emily. "We can puzzle it out over coffee." She was looking forward to the task of deciphering the note with the same enthusiasm she usually reserved for competitions.

Dear Mum and Dad,

This is to let you know that I am somewhere over the sea in Samuel Swain's shop. Miss Pryce and Miss Pryce are here as well. Can you send someone? Weather O.K. so far.

Your loving son,

Henry

P.S. Please excuse small writing.

"It doesn't make sense," said Albert, stirring cream into his coffee. "How can he be over the sea in some chap's shop? And who is this Samuel Swain? And who the thump are Miss Pryce and Miss Pryce? And what about this person he wants us to send? Who's that?"

Emily Hollins shook her head and tapped her pencil against her teeth, thoughtfully. "It's got me baffled," she said.

"Excuse me," said a voice at Albert's elbow.

Mr and Mrs Midgeley were having coffee at the adjoining table. It was Mr Midgeley who had spoken. "I'm sorry to be a nuisance," he went on, "but could I possibly trouble you for the sugar?"

"Of course," said Albert, handing over the sugar-bowl. "Be my guest."

"*Muchos gracias,*" said Mr Midgeley.

"I hope you won't think we're poking our long noses in where they're not wanted," began Mrs Midgeley, "but we couldn't help overhearing what you were saying."

"Oh?"

"Yes, about the Misses Pryce. You were wondering who they were? Well, they're the two sisters who usually sit at the table near the door in the dining-room."

"They both wear long black beads and glasses," added Mr Midgeley.

"Oh, yes!" said Emily. "You remember, Albert! That waitress was telling us about them—they went missing the same time as our Henry."

"Oh, *those* two!" said Albert. "They looked a couple of extremely nice ladies. If our Henry's with them, I should think we can relax—he must be in good hands."

Emily studied the note again, and frowned. "There's just this bit about being over the sea in somebody's shop that's puzzling me still—" She broke off as a smile crept over her face. "I think I've cracked it, Albert," she said.

"Go on."

"It's Henry's spelling, it never was up to much."

"How do you mean?"

"He doesn't mean 'shop' at all. He means '*ship*'. He's written 'o' instead of 'i'. 'I am somewhere over the sea in Samuel Swain's *ship*.' That's what he meant to write."

"Of course!" exclaimed Albert. "We've no need to worry at all then. He's gone off for a sail in this chap's boat. And these Pryce ladies have gone as well. All aboard the *Skylark*, eh? They'll probably be back any minute . . . There's just one thing left I *don't* understand."

"What's that, Albert?"

"Where he's written 'Can you send someone?' What do you

think he means by that?"

"Excuse me," said Mrs Midgeley, "and I hope you won't think we're interfering? But we might be able to shed some light on that problem."

"We'd be ever so grateful," said Emily.

Mrs Midgeley leaned even closer until her blue-rinsed hair came close to tickling Emily's nose. She ran her finger along Henry's writing. "Just here," she said, and read aloud: *"Miss Pryce and Miss Pryce are here as well. Can you send someone?"*

"What does it mean?" asked Albert.

"We do happen to know that the Misses Pryce had booked two seats for the Pier Theatre tonight," said Mr Midgeley. "They're to be picked up at the theatre box-office."

"Reggie and I went to the matinée last Saturday," said Mrs Midgeley. "It's a wonderful Star-Studded Entertainment, isn't it, Reg?"

"We thoroughly enjoyed ourselves," agreed her husband. "Do you know, there's a rather well-built lady who plays the accordion and gets the audience to sing-a-long with her—she ought to be on television!"

"She did, she did!" said Mrs Midgeley. "And there's a man who lies on his back and juggles things in the air with his feet!"

"Is there really?" said Emily, impressed. "I do wish we could have got tickets."

"That's what I'm coming to," said Mr Midgeley. "Referring back to the note from your son: *Can you send someone?* Do you suppose the Pryce sisters realized they couldn't get back from their boat trip in time for the show tonight, and didn't want to waste the tickets?"

"I suppose that's possible," said Albert, glancing at his wife.

"Well then," urged Mrs Midgeley, "why don't you take advantage and get along there yourselves?"

Mr Midgeley tugged at his gold watch-chain and his gold watch came out of his waistcoat pocket. "The curtain goes up in fifteen minutes—you'll just make it if you set off right away."

"Oh, Albert, do you think we could?"

"Well . . ."

"It'll take you out of yourselves," said Mr Midgeley.

"It will indeed!" agreed his wife. "There's a competition in the second half."

"A competition?" breathed Emily, excitedly.

"A talent competition," explained Mr Midgeley. "Vera was going to go in for it, weren't you, Vera? She was going to get up on the stage and sing *Rule Britannia*." He nodded at his wife's blue rinse. "She had her hair done specially."

"It's very nice," said Emily.

"Only she goes and gets stage fright at the very last minute—so she never went on!"

"Emily suffers from that," said Albert, then turning to his wife, he added: "That's one competition you *won't* be going in for!"

"Not me," said Emily. "But you could."

"What does he do?" asked Mr Midgeley.

"He puts his fingers in his mouth and does bird imitations."

"Are you any good?" Mrs Midgeley asked Albert.

"Not bad," he replied, modestly.

"If you're any good at all, you'll *walk* it. There's not much competition," said Mr Midgeley.

"What are we wasting time for?" said Albert Hollins. "Get your coat on, Emily."

"Are we really going?"

"I don't see why we shouldn't enjoy ourselves—now that we know young Henry's safe and sound."

The night was pitch-black and silent.

The storm had blown itself out and the Inflatable Shop was drifting, listing dangerously, in a starless sky.

Suddenly, there was an ominous squeaking from the mooring-ropes. The building shuddered and dropped another twelve centimetres at its lowest end.

"If it tips any more," said Mildred, rustling her jet-beads between her finger-tips, "we shall all slide off the side and into . . ." She paused, gulped, and look down over the veranda.

The terrible blackness of the night surrounded them and it was impossible to tell how far they were above the sea.

Samuel Swain flashed a powerful torch upwards in the direction of the inflatable goods that floated above the corrugated-iron roof.

His three companions held their breaths and cocked their ears for the tell-tale sound of escaping gas, for it was their captain's belief that they had sprung a leak.

"There it is—that's the one!" said Samuel, as the torch's beam picked out the largest, and farthest, of the dinghies swinging above their heads. It was already visibly deflated. And now their ears could just detect the faint hissing sound. "Must have took a puncture in the storm, I reckon," continued

Samuel. "Seems to be coming from somewhere up on top—right where we can't get at it."

"But the valve's down there, man!" objected Augusta, seizing the torch and pointing at the lower half of the dinghy. "Surely, all you need to do is blow more gas inside it?"

The old sailor shook his head. "The devilment of it is, ma'am, if I starts pumping gas into that there craft while she's still punctured—then the extra pressure could more than likely rip her more than ever."

"But if you *don't* put more gas in, you stupid man, it will deflate right down and we will be done for!"

As if to underline her statement, the mooring-ropes strained and squealed again and the shop settled down several more centimetres.

"What you're saying, captain," said Henry, "is that you can't pump any more gas into it until the puncture's mended?"

"Aye, shipmate, that's about the size of it."

"Goodness!" fretted Mildred. "Whatever are we going to *do*?"

"Think of something quickly, I sincerely hope!" said Augusta, flashing Samuel an icy glance. "It's your fault we're up here—haven't you got *anything* to suggest?"

"Supposing one of us went up there?" said Henry.

Mildred craned her neck and looked up at the mass of mooring-lines and guy-ropes that secured the inflated goods to the roof of the shop. "Wouldn't it be extremely dangerous to try to climb up those?"

"Yes," snapped Augusta. "But it would make more sense than standing about here doing nothing." She too gazed up at the criss-cross network of ropes. "It *should* be possible," she said, and then, looking straight at Henry, continued: "But if anyone *is* going up there, it would be best if it was someone *small*."

"I don't mind," said Henry.

"There ain't nobody going to climb them ropes," said Samuel, firmly. "Why—anybody clambering around up there would do more harm than good. Supposing their foot was to slip? It could go right through the side of any one o' them inflatables. Then where would we be?"

"No worse off than we are now," said Augusta, as the floor of the Inflatable Shop dipped again. Keeping her eyes still fixed on Henry, she continued: "*Someone* could go up in their stocking-feet."

"An' I say nobody's climbing them there ropes," said Samuel. "And them's orders!"

"Supposing," said Henry, "I went up there without using the ropes?"

Samuel smiled. "Sort of floated up there of your own accord, young 'un?"

But Henry wasn't joking. "Yes," he said, "I could put on a couple of swimming-rings and you could fill them with gas."

"Sink me," roared Samuel, "you *does* mean float up—an' it just might work at that!"

"I could put on some swimming arm-bands as well," said Henry.

The old sailor thumped his fist in his empty palm. "By thunder, lad, I reckon it *will* work, too! We'd need to put a line on you though, or you'd float away."

"What are we [illegible] for then?" snapped Augusta. "The shop's sinking by the [illegible]

"Have you got a punctu[illegible]" asked Henry.

"In the store-cupboard. In th[illegible]nd cubby-'ole, first shelf down."

"I'll get it," said Mildred.

In next to no time, Henry was fitted out w[illegible] rings and arm-bands. Captain Swain switched o[illegible] inflating apparatus and applied the nozzle to each of He[illegible] valves in turn.

Henry began to feel himself growing lighter and lighter.

"How does that feel, young 'un?" asked Samuel, making a final adjustment.

"About right, I think," said Henry, torch in one hand and puncture outfit in the other. "Try letting out some line and let's see how I go."

Samuel unfastened the end of the line that secured Henry to the veranda-rail and slowly—ever so slowly—began to pay it out. Henry felt himself taking off.

"Be careful, Henry," Matilda called up to him as he floated up towards the roof.

"Yes! Be *very* careful!" cried Augusta. "Especially where you put your feet!"

"I'm sure he'll do that without having to be told, Augusta," said Mildred.

"You may think so," said Augusta. "But I happen to *know* that all boys are extremely clumsy."

Henry had not heard this last exchange. Captain Swain had paid out a little more line than was necessary and Henry found

...nflatables on the roof
himself floating high above the top ...omfortably, arms and legs
of the shop. He settled there ... on the end of the line. He gazed
extended, and spinni... ...as very much to see. The night was so
around. Not th... ...as if he could almost reach out and grab a
...blackness.
dark ... like an astronaut who had got out of his space-capsule
...order to inspect his craft. Could this be what it would be like in space, he wondered? So very quiet and peaceful?

"Ahoy there, young 'un! You all right?"

The voice of Samuel Swain drifted up from the veranda.

"Crikey!" thought Henry. "This won't do! Astronauts don't spend their time day-dreaming—or is it *night*-dreaming? I'd better get on with the job." He glanced down at the deflating dinghy a metre or so below him. "Can you pull me in a bit?" he called.

Captain Swain hauled on the line and Henry swung down until his head was just above the top of the dinghy.

"Okay!" he yelled. "That's fine!"

He reached out his hand and allowed his fingers to run, gently, over the surface of the dinghy. He found the puncture almost immediately. He could feel the movement on his finger-tips as the gas hissed out of the tiny tear in the inflated boat.

"Got it!" he called down.

"Oh, well done, Henry!" shouted Mildred.

"Is it a big job?" cried Samuel.

"No! It's only a small hole—I'll have it fixed in a jiffy!"

"Mind you make a good job of it! Don't *rush* things!"

Augusta bellowed up at him, adding: "There's no sense in spoiling the ship for a ha'porth of tar!"

Up above the roof of the Inflatable Shop, Henry grinned to himself. "The funny thing is," he told himself, as he opened the puncture kit and balanced the box on top of the dinghy, "I'm quite enjoying all of this!"

Henry sang to himself as he went to work.

"Oh, I do like to be beside the seaside!

Oh, I do like to be beside the sea—

"Come along, everybody!" cried the well-built lady in the organdie dress as she swayed to-and-fro on the stage, her fingers roaming up and down the keys of her piano-accordion. "Sing up!" she called.

The packed audience in the Pier Theatre threw back their heads and joined her in song.

"Oh, I do like to stroll along the prom-prom-prom!

Where the brass-bands play tiddley-om-pom-pom!"

Only one member of that happy audience sat silent. Emily Hollins, Seat 28, Row J, stared straight ahead, her mouth shut.

"Come on, Emily—sing up!" whispered Albert, in the next seat, nudging her with his elbow. Accidentally however, he knocked over the box of soft-centred chocolates that she had balanced on the arm of her seat. The box tumbled to the floor, spilling chocolates in all directions.

Emily did not even seem to notice.

"What's the matter, Emily? What is it?" asked Albert, realizing that something was seriously wrong.

"Let's go," whispered Emily.

"But we haven't seen the conjuror yet! Or the man who juggles with his feet! And what about the talent competition? I've got my name down."

"I've just remembered something important, Albert," said Emily. "It's to do with that note from Henry."

"Won't it wait?"

"I'm sorry, Albert—but, no, it won't." Emily meant what she said.

Albert Hollins got to his feet. "Excuse me," he said to the grizzled white-bearded man who was sitting on his other side, "but could we get past, please?"

"Could ye no' bide your time a wee while till the braw lassie has finished her song?" snapped Hugo McMurdo. The cantankerous old Scot got to his feet and grudgingly allowed Albert and Emily to shuffle past.

"What did he say?" whispered Emily.

Albert, mystified, shook his head.

They stumbled off along the aisle towards where the *Exit* sign glowed at the back of the theatre.

"I'm sorry to drag you away, Albert," said Emily, as they trudged the length of the dark, deserted pier in the direction of the promenade. "But it suddenly occurred to me who that man is that Henry mentioned in his note—Samuel Swain."

"And who is he, when he's at home?"

"He's that fat sailor chap who sells blow-up boats and things on the prom."

"So what?" asked Albert. "I don't see why we had to leave in such a rush just because you've remembered that."

"But don't you see, Albert? Samuel Swain *has* got a *shop*—not a ship. And if our Henry is over the sea, somewhere, in a novelty-shop, it's not as if he'd gone for a sail in somebody's boat. I mean, a novelty-shop's hardly the thing you'd *choose* for your son to go gadding around the world in, is it?"

"You're right, Emily—it isn't."

They walked on in silence for some minutes. The only sound to be heard was that of their feet echoing on the wooden planking.

Then, for the sake of something to do, Albert put his fingers in his mouth, pursed his lips, and blew gently, doing his imitation of a seagull.

Out across the sea, a real seagull heard Albert's imitation and mistook it for the real thing. The seagull opened its beak and mournfully answered the call.

"I could have won that talent contest hands down," said Albert.

Emily did not reply. Quickening her step, she walked purposefully through the turnstiles and off the pier onto the promenade.

5

The body of Lord Trentchester lay sprawled on the library carpet. He was as dead as mutton. A blood-stained ornate oriental paper-knife was sticking out of his chest. The weekend guests at Trentchester Hall, who had all been summoned to the library, gazed down at the corpse in stunned silence.

"Every one of you had a motive to kill his lordship," said Detective Inspector Creeley, looking at them each in turn. "What we now have to discover is which one of you had the opportunity?" It was at this point that Greaves, the grey-haired butler, entered with a tray of drinks.

Police Sergeant Edgar Threadgold smiled to himself, knowingly, as he placed his detective novel face-down on his desk while he stirred sugar into his cocoa.

"It's obvious," he said to himself. "It was the butler that did it. That paper-knife is a red herring. His lordship wasn't stabbed to death at all. He was strangled in the summerhouse on the lawn. Greaves dragged the body into the library later on and *then* stuck the paper-knife in him to throw Creeley off the scent."

Sergeant Threadgold shook his head and sighed. It would

take Creeley the rest of the book to work out who had murdered Lord Trentchester. He, Edgar Threadgold, had solved the mystery halfway through Chapter Five! And he was just a uniformed policeman!

The police sergeant dipped a digestive biscuit into his cocoa. He was wasting his time, he thought—stuck here, night after night, behind the desk at Cockleton-on-Sea's only police station. Nothing ever happened in holiday resorts. People came to Cockleton-on-Sea to *enjoy* themselves, not to murder one another. He should have put in for a transfer to New Scotland Yard *ages* ago. He frowned as the bottom half of his digestive biscuit, becoming cocoa-logged, broke off and sank in the mug.

Edgar Threadgold was fishing bits of biscuit out of his cocoa with his ballpoint when Albert and Emily Hollins walked into the station.

"We want to report something missing," said Emily Hollins, firmly.

"Hang on a second," said the police sergeant, reaching for the report book, "while I sort myself out and find the right page."

He guessed that this complaint would be the same as all the others. Another horrifying tale of a suitcase left in the boot of a taxi-cab, or one more gruesome story concerning a wedding ring lost on the sands! That was another thing that was wrong with being a seaside copper: visitors were constantly losing their belongings and expecting him to find them.

Sergeant Threadgold found an empty page at last. "I'll need to know your names and addresses, first of all," he said.

"Mr and Mrs Albert Hollins," Albert told him, and then paused before continuing: "Do you mean the address we're staying at in Cockleton-on-Sea? Or do you mean our address when we're at home?"

"Both," said the police sergeant, with a sigh. And that was yet one more good reason for applying for an inland post—you invariably had to write down *two* addresses for almost everyone who came into a holiday resort police station. "And I shall want both of your telephone numbers as well," he added.

Later, when names, addresses, telephone numbers and all the rest of the relevant background information had been entered in the report-book, Sergeant Threadgold turned to the question of the incident itself. "Rightyho then," he began, sharpening his pencil, "and what exactly is it that you've lost? A wedding ring or a suitcase?"

"Neither," said Emily, "it's our son, Henry."

"Him and a shop," said Albert.

"H-i-m a-n-d a s-h-o—" The police sergeant, who had begun to write things down, reached for his rubber. "Just for a moment then, I thought you said a shop!"

"I did," said Albert.

"A novelty-shop," said Emily. "The one that sells blow-up boats and toys and things. It's run by an old sailor called Samuel Swain."

"I know the one," said Threadgold. "It's on the end of the promenade."

"It *was* on the end of the promenade," said Emily. "But it isn't there any longer. We've just looked."

"It's gone," said Albert. "The shop, our son, this chap

Swain—oh, and a couple of sisters by the name of Pryce. They've done a vanishing act as well."

"You don't suppose," said the police sergeant hopefully, thinking that there might be a bit of real excitement in Cockleton-on-Sea at last, "that there's any chance that it's been hijacked?"

"Why would anyone want to hijack a novelty-shop?" asked Albert.

Sergeant Threadgold shrugged. "You'd be surprised at some of the things the criminal fraternity gets up to these days," he said. "What would you say about a butler who strangled his employer, and then stuck a paper-knife into him afterwards to throw people off the scent?"

"Good gracious me!" said Emily. "Who's done that?"

The police sergeant tapped the side of his nose with his forefinger. "I'm afraid I'm not at liberty to divulge that information—yet." He changed the subject, hastily. "Going back to this shop of yours. Do you have any evidence to substantiate your claim?"

Emily opened her voluminous handbag and scuffled about among competition entry-forms. "There's this," she said, producing Henry's note.

Threadgold studied the document. "This looks pretty substantial," he said at last.

"Don't take our word for it," said Albert. "Go down to the promenade and take a look for yourself."

"What? And leave the station unattended? My superintendent would do his nut!"

"Haven't you got anyone you can send?" asked Emily.

Threadgold shook his head. "I'm completely on my own here every night. I work to a very strict routine. Constable Hopper goes off duty at eight p.m. when I come on. I'm stuck here till he comes on again at eight-fifteen in the morning. Subject to the arrival of young Hopper, my hands are tied."

"Very well," said Emily, taking a seat on a wooden bench, "if that's the case—we'll wait."

"All night?"

"If needs be," said Emily. "Albert, sit down."

Albert Hollins joined his wife on the bench.

The police sergeant recognized that Emily Hollins was a determined woman. "Very well, madam, if that is your decision. But I must ask you to remember that I have a job to do. Please don't get under my feet while I'm trying to effect the due processes of the law." He glanced up at the police-station clock.

It was exactly nine p.m.

Police Sergeant Threadgold worked to a strict routine and at exactly nine o'clock, every night, he fed the station cat. He glanced down under his desk and rubbed the tips of his fingers against his thumb. "Puss-puss-puss!" he called. "Here, pussykins!"

The sun crept over the horizon, stabbing its rosy fingers into a thin skein of low grey clouds along the horizon and casting a glow across the sea.

Inside the Inflatable Shop, Henry Hollins yawned, stretched, and clambered out of the makeshift bed he had fashioned for himself among some coils of rope in a dusty corner.

The others, he noticed, were still asleep.

Mildred and Augusta had spent the night on a pair of bunk-beds they had constructed by placing inflated air-mattresses on top of, and underneath, the counter. They had also found some large flags in the store-cupboard which they had used as blankets.

Mildred was tucked up, soundly, on the lower bunk, under the Union Jack. Augusta was lying on top of the counter beneath the flag of Wales across the centre of which there breathed a fiery dragon.

Samuel Swain was snoring, gently, in a rickety wooden chair, his hands folded over his ample stomach, his fingers interlocked.

Deciding to let them sleep, Henry tiptoed across the floor and stepped out onto the veranda.

He blinked in surprise.

The last time he had looked down in daylight, on the previous afternoon, the sea had stretched away on every glittering side, some hundreds of metres below. At this moment, it was heaving, ominously, no more than a metre below the spot where he stood. In fact, he realized, the occasional slopping sound that he could hear was caused by the ocean swell washing up beneath the floor of the shop.

Henry ran back inside and shook Samuel by the arm.

"Belay there, shipmate! What's amiss?" said the captain, opening one eye.

"We're almost in the sea, captain! It's just beneath the floor!"

Samuel was out on the veranda in a moment. "Swamp me,

young 'un!" he murmured, as the waters under them rose up again, slightly higher than before, sending up a shower of spray through the cracks between the floorboards. "By thunder, shipmate, we'll need to act at once if we're not to get a soaking!"

"What catastrophe have you brought down upon us now?" Augusta, having been wakened by the sound of the sea beneath the shop-floor, had got out of bed and joined them on the veranda.

"Now, now," said Samuel. "Nothing to concern yourself about, ma'am. We'll soon have the situation under control."

"A likely story!" snapped Augusta, as the sea fairly pounded up against the planking, sending another shower of icy spray that, this time, drenched them up to their knees.

"Mercy me!" gasped Mildred, joining them. "Are we sinking?"

"Not a bit of it, ma'am," said Samuel. "Keep calm. As I was just explaining to your sister, we 'ave everything in 'and."

"Indeed we have!" Augusta spoke bitterly. "Apart from being lost, nobody knows where, on a friendless sea—now it would appear we are about to drown in those self-same cruel waters!"

Samuel Swain shot Augusta a long, reproachful look. "As to the first part o' that statement, ma'am, regardin' bein' lost—well now, I 'as to admit to that bein' true. As to *why* we're lost, beggin' y'r pardon, but I seems to recollect a certain lady informin' the entire ship's company as to 'ow she was conversant with chartin' a course. A duty which I duly entrusted to 'er. Now, ma'am, is that or is it not the truth?"

And, for once in her life, Augusta was too embarrassed to reply.

"As to the second part of your statement, ma'am," continued Samuel, "regardin' this 'ere craft bein' about to go under—I don't 'old that to be true at all—"

"We do seem to be actually touching the water now," broke in Mildred, anxiously.

They all peered over the veranda. Mildred was right. The water level was rising up the side of the shop.

"Thank 'ee, ma'am, for keeping me so informed," said Samuel, politely.

"Then for goodness' sakes, man, *do* something," urged Augusta. "Put some more gas inside the inflatables! Get us up in the air again!"

"It's too late for that now, ma'am," said the captain. "What's wanted now is emergency action—the on'y thing that'll save us now is to lighten our load." And his eyes were on the Pryce sisters as he spoke.

"Heavens above," wailed Mildred, clinging to her sister's arm, "he's going to throw us over the side, Augusta! We'll be consumed by sharks!"

"Fiddle-faddle," said the elder of the two, and: "Pull yourself together, Mildred!"

Samuel Swain smiled and shook his head. "I'm goin' to *put* you over the side, ma'am—and on'y as a temporary measure." Then, turning to Henry, he continued: "Break out the lifeboat, lad—that big 'un that's been bouncin' about inside the cabin. Smartly does it, now!"

Henry darted inside the shop and returned, an instant later, dragging the large dinghy. Together the old sailor and the boy lowered the dinghy over the veranda and into the sea. Samuel tied the dinghy's painter to the veranda-rail.

"If you'll be so good as to give me your 'and, ma'am," said Samuel to Mildred, "I'll assist you into the boat."

"Are you sure it's safe?" asked Mildred, apprehensively.

"Safe as a toy-duck in a bath, ma'am!"

"Oh, tush, Mildred," said Augusta, impatiently. "I'll go first." And taking a firm grip of Samuel's hand she jumped, lightly, into the waiting dinghy.

Samuel turned to Mildred who was still hanging back. "Surely you ain't a-goin' to 'ave it said as 'ow your sister's braver than you are yourself, ma'am?"

Mildred shook her head. Summoning all her courage, accepting the offer of the captain's steadying hand, she joined Augusta in the dinghy.

"Well done, ma'am!" Samuel turned to Henry. "Now, young 'un, you an' me c'n pump a bit o' gas into the inflatables—enough to keep us on a steady course."

"Just be quick about it," snapped Augusta. "We've no wish to waste more time than is necessary in this small boat."

"I was wonderin', ma'am, whether you an' your sister might consider doin' us all a service," Samuel gave Henry a sly wink as he continued, "rather than waste your time entirely while you're in that there dinghy."

"What sort of service?" asked Augusta, suspiciously.

"I was thinkin' pertickerly of a spot o' rowin', ma'am."

"*Rowing?*" Augusta echoed, astounded.

"This 'ere shop bein' down near the sea could turn out to be a blessin'—not a 'andicap," said Samuel. "I was thinkin' as 'ow some on us could have a spell, turn and turn about, at takin' the oars an' rowin' us back to port."

"Rowing!" gasped Augusta, yet again.

"Before breakfast?" enquired Mildred, unhappily.

"There's nothing like a spot o' rowin' for workin' up a h'appetite." Samuel turned to Henry. "Nip inside again, young 'un, and fetch out those oars as is 'anging up behind the store-cupboard."

Henry did as he was told.

"But what's the point of rowing anywhere without charts or compass?" argued Augusta.

"I don't make no claims to bein' a navigator—like some folks does as I could name but won't. But I recognizes that when I sees it." Samuel pointed across at the red ball of the sun which had now climbed above the rim of the horizon. "I reckons if we was to steer a course, keepin' that there sun behind our left shoulder, we must be makin' towards 'ome, give or take a mile or two."

Henry returned carrying the two pairs of oars that went with the dinghy. He handed the oars to Samuel who passed them down to the Pryce sisters.

"They fits snug in them rowlocks near your elbows, ladies," said Samuel.

"But what about breakfast?" mumbled Mildred.

"I'm sure the young 'un 'ere'll be more'n 'appy to relieve you for a spell, ma'am, shortly. You c'n 'op aboard then an' prepare a bite for us all. We collected a deal o' rain-water in that sheet I set up last night. I reckons a nice 'ot cup o' tea an' a similarly

nice 'ot bowl o' Mulligatawny soup wouldn't go down 'alf bad on a morning such as this."

"And when, may I ask, is it *your* intention to take a turn at the oars?" asked the tight-lipped Augusta.

"Well now, ma'am," said Samuel, with the hint of a smile at the corners of his mouth, "as I've willingly admitted, I ain't no dab-'and maritime navigator—but in the entire absence o' anyone else o' that perfession, I reckons it's up to me to stay on board this craft an' see as 'ow we 'olds a steady course, like." With which, Samuel Swain saluted the ladies, smartly, and took up a position on the veranda.

Mildred and Augusta Pryce took up their oars and bent their backs to the task. Their black beads rattled in unison as they pulled the dinghy slowly across the sea. Behind them they towed the Inflatable Shop.

Captain Swain turned to Henry Hollins. "Well, shipmate, we're on our way, I reckons."

"Yes, captain, but are you quite sure we're heading in the right direction?"

"That, young 'un," said Samuel, lowering his voice so as not to be overheard by the ladies, "remains to be seen."

Police Sergeant Edgar Threadgold tugged at the oars, slipped on his seat, and tumbled backwards into the bottom of the rowing-boat, losing his helmet in the fall.

"I shouldn't be doing this job," he grumbled to himself as he scrambled back into position. "They ought to have sent a coastguard or somebody from the Harbour Police!" He stabbed the oars into the sea again and the boat spun round, haphazardly. "On the other hand," he told himself, "if I solve this one, it could lead to promotion. *The Curious Case of the Disappearing Novelty-Shop*, that's what they'll call it. No, I shouldn't complain—I've been waiting years for a job like this to drop into my lap!" He tried to concentrate on steering the rowing-boat towards the fishing-boat that was chugging in his direction.

"*Highland Lassie*, ahoy!" yelled the police sergeant.

"Och, mon, get oot o' ma' way!" Hugo McMurdo called back at him from the wheelhouse window.

As the rowing-boat drew level with the *Highland Lassie*, Sergeant Threadgold stumbled to his feet and grabbed at the side of the fishing-boat. Throstlethwaite looked up briefly from his work and then decided to mind his own business. Sergeant Threadgold clung there, unsteadily, his feet still in the rowing-boat, his head and shoulders level with the deck of the larger craft.

"I am a police officer and I have the authority to hold your vessel in port if need be," he called out to the old Scots skipper as the fishing-boat steamed slowly on towards the harbour entrance.

"And I'm the skipper of it, mon," McMurdo yelled back, "and ye'll not tell Hugo McMurdo when he can take his boat oot or no!"

By now, Sergeant Threadgold had succeeded in scrambling up onto the deck of the *Highland Lassie*. He clambered to his feet and dusted fish-scales off his uniform.

"I understand," he called across to the wheelhouse, "that you have a Mr Frank Throstlethwaite aboard this vessel?"

"Aye. That's yer mon, working there."

Threadgold looked at where McMurdo's bony finger was pointing and saw the bosun in the prow of the boat, mending a fishing net.

"Whisht! Awa' there, bosun!" McMurdo bellowed in his thick Highland brogue. "There's a mon here frae the police hoose tae see ye!"

"Sorry, skipper!" The bosun yelled back. "What did you say?"

"Och, awa' an' talk to him yersel', mon," grumbled the skipper to the police sergeant. "An' be sure tae speak up loud an' a'—the mon's as deef as a post."

"I'm much obliged to you, skipper," said Sergeant Threadgold, touching the brim of his helmet.

"An' ah'll be obliged to ye', if ye' dinna tak' tae lang aboot y'r business. Ah hae to mak' a livin', mon."

Threadgold nodded and picked his way across the coils of rope and stacks of baskets to where the bosun was working.

"MR THROSTLETHWAITE, I BELIEVE!" bellowed the police sergeant in the bosun's ear.

The bosun almost jumped out of his skin. "There's no need to shout—I'm not deaf."

"Sorry," said Threadgold. "I thought you were." The police sergeant referred to his notebook. "I am conducting an investigation, sir, into the disappearance of an entire retail establishment from off the promenade."

"Search me if you like," joked the bosun. "I haven't got it."

"Perhaps not, sir," said the police sergeant, in no mood for jokes. "But I believe you are familiar with this?" He had taken Henry's note out of his pocket and now showed it to the bosun.

Frank Throstlethwaite glanced across at the wheelhouse, nervously. If he owned up to recognizing the note, he would be in trouble with his skipper for not having thrown it back in the sea. The wrath of the cantankerous Hugo McMurdo would descend upon him in no uncertain manner. Luckily, McMurdo's attention was elsewhere.

"I've never seen it before in all my life," said the bosun.

The police sergeant's mouth dropped open. "Are you absolutely sure?"

"Positive," said the bosun, firmly. He was beginning to enjoy pulling the wool over the police sergeant's eyes. "In fact," he added, "I've never even seen anything remotely like it."

Police Sergeant Threadgold blew out his cheeks and stuffed the note back in his pocket. Here was a pretty kettle of fish! The couple who'd spent the night in the police station had obviously got their facts wrong. He had had a wasted trip out to the fishing-boat. There was nothing for it now but to row himself back to the shore again.

Threadgold turned to leave—and realized that the fishing-boat was under way. They had already left the calm waters of the bay and were out into the choppy sea beyond the harbour wall. Looking back into the harbour, he could just see his rowing-boat, unattended and drifting aimlessly.

He hurried across and hammered on the wheelhouse door with his fists. "What's going on?" he yelled. "Turn this boat back, you silly old fool!"

The door opened several centimetres and McMurdo stuck his nose out. "Ah tell't ye ah'd nae time tae hang aboot! Time, tide and Hugo McMurdo wait fer nae mon!"

"I demand that you turn this boat about immediately and put me back in port!" insisted the police sergeant. "Otherwise I shall arrest you for kidnapping a police officer!"

"Hoots, mon—awa' wi' ye!" crowed the old Scot. "It's yoursel' that's breaking the law, mon! Stowin' awa's an offence against the Maritime Code the noo!"

"Me?" gasped the police sergeant. "A stowawa'? I mean, a stowaway?"

"Aye!" The gnarled old skipper cackled mischievously. "An' stowawa's on mah boat hae to earn their keep, mon. Get yoursel' up forrard and gi' the bosun a hand to stow the gear awa'—we're off tae sea!" With which, McMurdo slammed the door.

"Hang on! Just a minute!" called the police sergeant, rattling the brass ring on the wheelhouse door.

But McMurdo had bolted the wheelhouse on the inside and was concentrating all of his attention on steering the boat.

Police Sergeant Threadgold clutched at his helmet and grabbed the deck-rail for support as the *Highland Lassie*'s bows dipped sharply as she hit the open sea.

6

In out . . . In out,

In out . . . In out . . .

Henry Hollins and Samuel Swain matched each other, stroke for stroke, as they heaved on the oars. The dinghy ploughed on through the ocean, towing in its wake the Inflatable Shop.

Henry and Samuel had relieved the Pryce sisters in the dinghy some time before.

Mildred was preparing a mid-morning meal and the tantalizing smell of Mulligatawny soup drifted out through the open window.

Augusta was striding up and down the veranda with the captain's telescope tucked under one arm and clearly enjoying her temporary role as master of the craft. Occasionally, she would raise the glass to her eye and scan the horizon with a broad sweep.

"She can't do no damage, young 'un," whispered Samuel. "She can't get us no more lost than we are already."

"Haven't you *any* idea where we are, captain?"

"Not so much as a whisper of it, shipmate." Samuel Swain spoke cheerfully. He paused and looked around at the sea before continuing. "But I reckons goin' anywhere is preferable to sittin' where you are an' goin' nowheres at all! Backs to it, young 'un!"

There was a silence for several minutes as they both applied themselves to the oars.

"Elevenses are served!" called Mildred, stepping out onto the veranda.

"Dang me, ma'am, if I won't make a sailor of you yet!" cried Samuel, shipping his oar.

Henry did the same, and then followed the captain up onto the veranda.

"Well, ma'am," said Samuel, sniffing the aroma that was coming from the window. "An' what sort o' vittals are you offerin' us? Roast beef and Yorkshire pudden, is it? Or a 'andy portion o' steak-and-kidney pie?"

"I'm afraid it's only Mulligatawny soup, captain," said Mildred, a trifle nervously.

"Mulligatawny soup!" roared Samuel. "Why, ma'am, I'll be a cross-eyed ship's carpenter's uncle, if you ain't pervided us with the favourite dish of every sailorman from Madagascar to the Bay of Biscay!"

Mildred flushed, proudly. "Have I really?" she said.

Samuel clapped an arm around Henry's shoulders. "Come on, young 'un," he cried. "Mulligatawny soup is not a dish best served by bein' allowed to stand around an' go cold. You too, ma'am," he added, turning to Augusta.

But Augusta had not heard. She was standing quite still with the telescope clapped to one eye.

"Land!" she cried. "Land ahoy!"

"What's that, ma'am?"

"*Land*," she repeated, firmly. "Land off the port bow, I believe is the correct nautical expression."

Samuel snatched the telescope from her and focused it in the direction she was pointing. "Swamp me, shipmates," he cried. "She's right! It *is* land!"

"Do you recognize the coastline?" asked Augusta. "Do you know now where we are?"

Samuel shook his head. He was squinting through the eyepiece at a thin line of pure white sand and a long stretch of unfriendly-looking jagged rocks beyond the beach. There was no sign of human life or even of vegetation.

"It ain't Cockleton-on-Sea, an' that is a fack," said Samuel, softly, snapping shut the telescope. "An' I can't tell from 'ere whether it be a long stretch o' coastline or no more'n a titchy little island."

"There's only one thing for it then," said Augusta.

"An' what might that be, ma'am?"

"Why—we must row there with all speed."

"Beggin' y'r pardon, ma'am," said Samuel, touching the brim of his cap with his forefinger. "But that ain't the way that I sees the situation at all."

"Oh?" Augusta's voice was icy cold. "And what might you propose?"

"Well, now, it seems to me as 'ow that there land ain't a-goin' to up and off if we leaves it there awhile. On the other 'and, we've got them bowls o' soup inside the shop. I'm proposin', ma'am, that we spoons some warmin' vittals into our stummicks first—then sets out to investigate that coast."

"You stupid man," stormed Augusta. "We could get off this silly shop, enjoy hot baths, clean clothes *and* what's more . . ." She paused and glowered at her sister before continuing: "have a *proper* meal instead of sharing a tin of soup!"

"It isn't my fault that there's only soup on board," snapped Mildred. "At least I tried to do *something* to help, instead of just walking up and down with a telescope—"

"Who was it, I'd like to know," demanded Augusta, interrupting her sister, "who *saw* the land in the first place? If I hadn't been looking through the telescope—"

"Ladies, ladies!" said Samuel, wagging his finger at the sisters. "I'm sure if rescue *is* close at 'and, we ought be complimentin' each other—for every one on us 'as done his or her share to bring it about."

"What do you mean '*if*'?" asked Augusta, sharply. "We *are* about to be rescued, aren't we?"

Samuel shrugged, awkwardly. "That remains to be seen, ma'am. That's an unfamiliar coastline off our bows . . ."

"What you are saying, is that we may be no better off than we were before?"

"Not at all, ma'am—"

"Yes, you *are*!" said Augusta, cutting him short. "You don't know where we are! You don't know what that land might be!" She stamped her foot on the veranda planking. "You call yourself the captain but, because of your incompetence, we could be *anywhere*! Why—for all you know, we might have been whisked off while we were asleep last night to another *planet*!"

"I 'ardly think *that's* possible, ma'am," said Samuel.

"But it's not *impossible*, is it? Great heavens, this whole experience seems hardly possible—but here we are to prove it! There was a terrible wind last night—we *could* have been whirled anywhere!" She paused and pointed across at the strip of land. "For all we know, that place might be inhabited by alien creatures with green bodies, three eyes, and antennae sticking up out of their heads!"

"Oh, goodness, Augusta," wailed her sister, "do you really think so?"

Samuel Swain smiled and shook his head. "There's no sense in getting 'ysterical, ladies. That's *land*, that is—an' that's the most important thing. So why don't we celebrate in style, eh? We could open up that family-size tin o' Treacle Pudding—that'd round off the Mulligatawny nicely." He placed a comforting arm around each of their shoulders. "Come on indoors an' we'll tackle that coastline later," he said, soothingly, and led them both inside the shop.

Henry hung back on the veranda for a moment. He gazed across at the empty coastline in which direction they were drifting closer minute by minute.

It was, without question, an unfriendly-looking sort of place. The pure white sand. The jagged rocks. The complete absence of any sign of life. The sun had disappeared behind a bank of cloud, casting the strip of land, the sea, and even the veranda on which he stood, in cold grey shadow.

Henry shivered—and followed his fellow-travellers inside.

As the shop-door closed behind him, there was a total stillness for several seconds. Not even a ripple disturbed the surface of the sea. Then, across on the land, a curious creature suddenly popped up from behind a rock and stared across at the Inflatable Shop.

The creature, although man-like in shape, had three eyes and a pair of quivering antennae on its hairless head. Its skin was a deep shade of green. It was dressed in a metallic silver one-piece suit and clutched a deadly-looking laser-type weapon in one of its three-fingered hands.

The creature gestured back, the way it had come, and its antennae twitched, violently, as it was joined by a similarly armed three-eyed green companion.

And then these two were joined by a third, and yet another—and then several more, all chattering excitedly.

Police Superintendent Horace Ampleforth smiled, proudly, at the framed photograph of himself on his desk-top. The photograph showed him holding a small silver cup, the Second Prize in the District Police Gardening Show, Red Cabbage class. The first prize for the best red cabbage had been a *large* silver cup and it had been won by Police Constable Ashley Hopper.

The superintendent allowed the smile to fade from his face as he took his eyes off the photograph and looked at the young constable on the other side of his desk.

"Yes, Hopper," said the superintendent. "What is it?"

"I've got today's incident-reports for you," said the young copper, brandishing a sheaf of papers.

Ampleforth sighed. He disliked incident reports. His whole life, it seemed, was spent listening to Constable Hopper reading out boring incident reports.

The superintendent leaned back in his swivel-chair and gazed up at the ceiling. "Carry on, Hopper," he said.

Constable Hopper cleared his throat and studied the top sheet on the pile. "There's a Mrs Delia Castle, staying at the Fredna Private Hotel, who's reported the loss of her wedding ring, Super. She thinks she lost it while sun-bathing on the beach."

"Next," and the superintendent blew out his cheeks and yawned.

"There's a Mr and Mrs Sumner Raistrick, staying at the Buona Vista boarding house, who have reported the loss of a suitcase. They think they left it in the boot of a taxi . . ."

As Constable Hopper's voice droned on, the superintendent closed his eyes and allowed his mind to wander. He thought about the red cabbages he would grow one day. Red cabbages as big as huge balloons, with purple outer leaves as smooth to the touch as velvet . . .

Hopper paused, and the superintendent blinked. "Is that the lot for today then, Hopper?"

"That's it, sir—" He hesitated, then: "Well, there is this one that Sergeant Threadgold filled in last night."

"Go on."

Constable Hopper cleared his throat again. "It's to do with a Mr and Mrs Albert Hollins, Super. They're staying at the Sea View hotel. They've reported the disappearance of a small shop."

"Pardon?"

"A small shop, Super. It's disappeared from the promenade."

Horace Ampleforth sat up in his chair.

"As a matter of fact, sir, it was a novelty-shop. The one just past the South Pier. You know the one, sir, it sold blow-up boats and that sort of thing. And some people have vanished too, sir, that were in it at the time."

"What people?"

"The eleven-year-old son of this Hollins couple. Also a chap called Swain who owns the shop. And a couple of sisters by the name of Pryce—they're staying at the same hotel as the Hollins family."

"That's a bit of an odd coincidence," said the superintendent. "It might be a good idea if we had the Hollins couple in for questioning."

"They are in, sir. They were here all night. Sergeant Threadgold sent them off to get some breakfast and told them to report back later. They're here now."

"And is Threadgold here as well?"

"That's where the plot thickens, Super, as they say in detective stories. Sergeant Threadgold's disappeared as well."

"Great Scott!"

"We had a call from the harbour-master, sir, about half an hour ago. It seems the sergeant borrowed his boat this morning to row out and interview somebody. The rowing-boat's turned up again—empty. There's no sign anywhere of Sergeant Threadgold."

Superintendent Ampleforth pursed his lips. "I think it's high time we started our own investigation. Ask Mr and Mrs Hollins to step in here."

"Very good, sir."

The young copper left the room and, a moment later, Albert and Emily Hollins walked through the door.

"Good morning," said the superintendent, holding out his hand to Albert. "I understand that you may be able to help us with our enquiries?"

The suspects had been herded together in the panelled library at Trentchester Towers. They watched, in silence, as Detective Inspector Creeley locked the library doors and filled his briar-pipe from his tobacco-pouch.

Creeley allowed his eyes to flicker around the room, taking in the suspects, one by one.

Count Rudolph von Hamburger, the wealthy German art-dealer, was polishing his monocle with a monogrammed silk handkerchief. Sally-Mae Masserling, the famous Hollywood film-star, was freshening her make-up. Timothy Trentchester, the ne'er-do-well young heir to the murdered lord's title, was examining his finger-nails. Algernon Dodd, the Trentchester family's decrepit old solicitor, was sorting out papers in his brief-case. Elspeth Minster-Lapwing, the international show-jumper, was fiddling with her riding-crop. Greaves, the balding butler, was toying, nervously, with the stopper of a cut-glass wine-decanter.

"This may come as a shock to most of you," began the New Scotland Yard detective, putting a match to his pipe and puffing for a few seconds before continuing, "but the murderer is not Greaves the butler."

"Well, I'm blowed!" murmured Police Sergeant Edgar Threadgold. "It certainly comes as a shock to me!" And he shook his head in disbelief as he glanced up from his paperback whodunnit and glanced over the side of the *Highland Lassie* at the rolling sea.

Hugo McMurdo was busy in the wheelhouse. Frank Throstlethwaite was down in the hold. The police sergeant was taking the opportunity to sit down in the stern of the boat and finish his book.

The news of Greaves' innocence flabbergasted him. He had plumped for the butler as the murderer as long ago as Chapter Five. Everything that he had read since then had only served to confirm his theory. What about the mud on Greaves' patent-leather shoes in Chapter Six? What about the incriminating book-match-cover in Chapter Eight? And what about the tell-tale cigarette-butt in the butler's pantry in Chapter Nine? And now, on the last page but one, here was that silly know-it-all, Detective Inspector Creeley, announcing that it wasn't Greaves that had done it after all!

Who *was* the murderer then? The wealthy German art-dealer? The ne'er-do-well son-and-heir? The doddering solicitor? Edgar Threadgold hastily turned the last page and began to read:

"*The truth of the matter is,*" *said Detective Inspector Creeley, pausing to savour the aroma of his pipe-tobacco, that Lord Trentchester was murdered by—*

At that precise moment, the paperback was snatched out of Threadgold's hands. He glanced up, in utter astonishment, in time to see his copy of *Who Killed His Lordship*? sailing through the air into the sea.

"Ah tell't ye ah've nae room aboard mah vessel for idle stowawa's, mon!" snapped Hugo McMurdo. It was the bad-tempered skipper himself who had hurled Threadgold's book into the sea.

"That's *stealing*, that is!" gasped the outraged police sergeant. "It's taking away personal private property without the owner's consent!"

"Nae, it's nae, mon."

"Yes, it is," insisted Threadgold. "It's a criminal offence!"

"Ah've nae taken it for ma' own use—ah've thrown it over the side. Aye—an' ah'll throw you after it too, mon, if ye dinna pick up that brush an' get to work on scrubbin' this deck doon!" With which dark threat, the old Scot turned on his gum-booted heel and stomped off into the wheelhouse.

Threadgold's mouth dropped open in astonishment. "Did you hear what he just said to me?" he enquired of the bosun, who was on his way out of the hold.

Throstlethwaite shook his head, gloomily. "I can never understand a word he says. If you want my opinion though, he's going round the twist. It's his age, you know—he's getting past it."

With which, the bosun moved off along the deck.

Sergeant Threadgold shook his head and wondered what he had got himself into this time. He patted his tunic pocket. The curious note about the missing novelty-shop was still safely tucked away. He had no intention of giving up on the job. What did it say, now? *I am somewhere over the sea in Samuel Swain's shop*. He would never know now who had murdered Lord Trentchester—but he certainly intended solving this mystery.

The police sergeant gazed around at the boundless ocean. There was not a novelty-shop in sight.

Then, catching a glimpse of Hugo McMurdo glowering at him through the wheelhouse window, Threadgold picked up the brush and made a show of scrubbing down the deck.

Henry Hollins slipped over the side of the dinghy and was pleased to feel firm sand between his toes. He had taken off his shoes, knotted the laces together, and hung them round his neck.

Mildred Pryce had left her shoes in the bottom of the dinghy and tucked up the bottom of her dress before she too slipped over the side and into the knee-deep water.

Together, Henry and Mildred took hold of the dinghy and towed it towards the beach, with the Inflatable Shop drifting along behind.

"Easy does it, shipmates!" called Captain Swain from the veranda. "Take her in gently, now!"

"It is absolutely ridiculous for a woman of her years to go paddling in the sea!" snapped Augusta, disapprovingly. "She'll probably catch her death of cold."

"No such thing, ma'am," snorted Samuel. "I never 'eard of anyone as suffered anything from splashing about in the ocean—unless, o' course, they couldn't swim an' it came up over their ears."

Henry and Mildred pulled the dinghy out of the sea and far enough along the dry white sand until the Inflatable Shop was floating, gently, just above the beach.

"How's that, captain?" called Henry.

Samuel glanced down over the veranda and took stock of the shop's position. "Entirely ship-shape, young 'un!" he shouted back. "The tide's up now as far as it's likely to come—I reckon she's safe enough for the time being!"

"What would you like us to do next?" called Mildred.

"Put your shoes and stockings on, I should imagine," muttered Augusta to herself, "and stop behaving like a silly schoolgirl."

Samuel silenced her with a glance. "Why, ma'am," he called down to Mildred, "if you an' the lad c'n just 'old 'er steady, I'll let some o' the gas out o' these inflatables an' set 'er down on dry land at least."

"Aye-aye, captain!" Mildred cried back, dusting the sand from her feet and slipping on her shoes. "Come along, Henry."

Captain Swain turned on the veranda to find himself confronted by a frowning Augusta. "Are you proposing," she began, "to set us down before we've even explored the area?"

"Exactly that, ma'am. For I don't see as 'ow any of us c'n go off explorin' and leave the shop up in the air—at the mercy o' any stray wind that might 'appen along."

"Supposing we need to leave in a hurry?" said Augusta.

"And why should we want to do that, ma'am?"

"I don't know . . ." Augusta turned her eyes towards the ridge of rocks that lay beyond the strip of sand. "I *do* know that I've got a funny feeling that we're being watched."

Samuel Swain followed her glance. He too had a strange foreboding that the strip of land was not as deserted as it seemed to be—but he shrugged off the thought. "All I knows, ma'am," he said, "is that this 'ere shop was allus intended as a shore-based establishment—would you go along with that?"

"I suppose so . . ." she agreed, reluctantly.

"An' you won't argue with me neither when I says it's served us well both as an air-ship an' also as a sort o' sea-going vessel?"

"That," said Augusta, coldly, "is a matter of opinion."

"No, ma'am, it ain't nothin' o' the kind!" Samuel spoke quite sharply. "It is an irrefutable fack, ma'am! An' we are all four on us alive an' kickin' now as testimony to it! On'y, speaking as master o' this vessel, I wouldn't care to make no promises with regard to it gettin' us anywheres else in the immediate future—not without *some* sort o' overhaul afore we sets off again. *That's* why I'm proposin' to set 'er down." Then, curtly dismissing Augusta, Samuel turned away and called back over the veranda rail to Henry and Mildred. "'Old 'er steady as she goes, shipmates—I'm about to beach 'er now!"

"Aye-aye, captain!" they called back in unison.

Henry Hollins and Mildred Pryce took a firm hold of either end of the veranda and held it steady while Samuel moved round opening various valves and letting out equal quantities of gas. Gradually, centimetre by centimetre, the Inflatable Shop sank down until, at last, it was resting safe and snug and squarely on the sand.

"Well done, shipmates!" Samuel shouted down to his assistants on the beach. "And now, if you'll join me back on board, I reckons our next job is to inspect all the inflatables outside for leaks an' tears or other signs o' damage."

Henry and Mildred got up onto the veranda.

Overhauling the Inflatable Shop was a job that would obviously take some time. While they were occupied, Augusta

decided that she had better make some show, at least, of sweeping out and tidying up the inside of the shop. It was, perhaps, because they were so busily at work, that the crew and captain of the travelling shop failed to notice the activity over by the rocks.

There were now some twenty or so of the alien creatures

peering across at the curious craft beached on the sea-shore. Three eyes blinked, inquisitively, out of each green face and a pair of antennae twitched on top of every shining bald head. They began to chatter to one another, excitedly, until one of their number, the tallest of the group, silenced them with a wave of a three-fingered hand.

This tallest creature, dressed in a grander uniform than his companions and obviously their leader, glanced back down the rise beyond the rocks to where a gigantic, glistening, circular interplanetary space-craft lay at rest. No sound came from the vessel but a myriad different coloured lights flickered on and off in the vast dome of its control room.

A hatch slid open, silently, in the lower half of the space-craft and twenty more of the green aliens poured out, all carrying laser-weapons. Then, at a hand sign from the tall one, these fresh reinforcements started up the rise to swell the ranks of their fellows behind the rocks.

Back at the Inflatable Shop, the four travellers applied themselves to the task of overhauling their grounded craft, oblivious to the fact that they were now outnumbered ten to one by green-skinned three-eyed aliens.

7

Study carefully the picture of the Zoo which our artist has drawn on the opposite page. He has hidden a number of animals in the illustration. How many of the following can you find? Four cuddly pandas; four pet bunnies; three furry guinea-pigs; a friendly zoo-keeper.

Emily Hollins put down the children's page of the newspaper and looked across the dining-room table at her husband, Albert. "It's no good," she said. "I've only found *two* cuddly pandas and one furry guinea-pig. I can't seem to concentrate at all."

Albert Hollins gave his wife a sympathetic smile. "Try not to worry about our Henry, Emily. I'm sure he'll turn up some time today. Why don't you try a mouthful of your prawn cocktail starter? You only get it once, you know. They won't put them on the menu again this holiday."

"No, thank you, Albert." Emily shook her head.

"Excuse me," said a voice at Emily's elbow, "but do you think we might bother you for the cruet?"

"No bother at all," said Emily, turning and passing the plastic salt-pepper-and-mustard-set to Mr Midgeley.

"I hope you won't think we're sticking our oar in where it isn't wanted," said Mrs Midgeley, "but we couldn't help overhearing—isn't there any news yet then, regarding your little boy?"

"None whatsoever, I'm afraid," said Albert.

"You know what they say," said Mr Midgeley, consolingly. "No news is good news."

"Every cloud has a silver lining," added his blue-rinsed wife.

"Actually," said Mr Midgeley, proffering Emily a newspaper, "we were wondering if you'd seen a copy of the mid-day edition of the *Cockleton-on-Sea Telegraph and Argus*?"

"We've got one, thank you," said Emily, holding up her own newspaper.

"Haven't you looked at the front page yet?" asked Mr Midgeley.

Emily shook her head. "I always turn to the competitions first."

"Why?" asked Albert. "What's on the front page?"

"It's all about your little boy and that shop," said Mr Midgeley.

Albert snatched the paper from Mr Midgeley while Emily refolded her own copy.

In the very centre of the front page was a large picture of the vacant space on the promenade left by the missing shop. Underneath this picture was a photograph of Police Sergeant Threadgold. Above the promenade picture, in big black letters, it said:

MYSTERIOUS DISAPPEARANCE OF LOCAL SHOP

And underneath the photograph of the police sergeant, in only slightly smaller letters, it said:

LOCAL MAN INVESTIGATES

Both Albert and Emily read on:

Police Sergeant Edgar Threadgold, aged 35, of Cockleton-on-Sea, is leading the investigations into the mysterious disappearance of a local shop from the promenade yesterday afternoon. Mrs Gracie Threadgold, the police sergeant's wife and herself a local woman, when interviewed this morning, told our reporter that her husband is a keen supporter of Cockleton-on-Sea Football Club and an avid reader of detective novels. Samuel Swain, the owner of the missing shop, has disappeared along with his business. Mr Swain, also a local man, lives alone at Seadrift Cottage, Old Bay Walk. His next-door neighbour, Mrs Eliza Dunwoody, another local woman, said this morning that Mr Swain is an ex-seafaring-man and that his principal hobbies are collecting driftwood and putting model ships in bottles. Also missing in the mysterious disappearance are three visitors to the town: Miss Augusta Pryce, Miss Mildred Pryce and Master Henry Hollings.

"It doesn't say much about Henry," objected Emily.

"That's probably because we're not local," said Albert.

"And they've spelled his name wrong," said Emily, biting her lip and wondering when she would see her only son again.

"What did you think of the show last night then?" said Mr Midgeley, thinking that it might be a good idea to change the subject.

"Oh, excellent!" said Albert. "Very good."

"And how did you get on in the talent competition?"

Albert shook his head. "I didn't go in for it, worse luck," he said. "We had to leave early. But we thought the lady with the piano-accordion was in a class of her own. Didn't we, Emily?"

Emily Hollins sniffed, nodded, and brightened a little. "Mmmm," she murmured. "We thoroughly enjoyed ourselves."

"We knew you would," said Mr Midgeley, handing back the plastic cruet-stand. *"Danke schön,"* he said.

As they sat over coffee, later, Emily could not help glancing occasionally at the photograph of Police Sergeant Threadgold.

She recollected the meeting with him in the police station the night before. He had *seemed* like a nice man. She was sure he was a keen and dedicated policeman. She hoped that Police Sergeant Threadgold was having some success in tracing the absent shop and her missing son . . .

"Och awa'!" grumbled Hugo McMurdo to himself, staring out through the spray-lashed wheelhouse window at the police sergeant. "Yon mon's nae more use than last year's haggis!"

Threadgold had been told to assist the bosun with the newly landed catch, but because of his heavily studded policeman's boots he was slipping and sliding all over the deck.

Edgar Threadgold was doing his best, but his boots were not his only handicap. A thick blue-serge policeman's uniform is not the best of clothing in which to load lively tail-slapping mackerel into wicker baskets. And every time the police sergeant bent down to pick up a fish, his helmet either fell down

over his eyes or dropped off altogether.

"Whoops-a-daisy!" gasped the startled police sergeant, as he skidded for the umpteenth time. He grabbed at the bosun to regain his balance but succeeded only in dragging the luckless Throstlethwaite onto the deck with him..

McMurdo could stand it no longer. "Hoots, mon!" he bellowed, poking his head out of the wheelhouse window.

"Can the twa' of ye nae stan' up on the legs the guid God gi' ye, wi'oot twirlin' roond and roond like a couple o' daft lassies!"

"I beg your pardon, skipper?" called the bosun, clambering to his feet and removing a mackerel that had somehow got lodged between his neck and the collar of his oilskin.

"Lord help us!" moaned McMurdo to himself. "One o' 'em's as daft as a brush an' the other one's as deef as a post!" Then, snatching up a length of ship's rope, the skipper lashed the wheel to hold its course, pushed open the wheelhouse door and made his way along the pitching deck. "Hoots, mon!" he yelled at the police sergeant who was struggling, yet again, to find his feet. "Ye're more hindrance than help, an' that's a fact!"

"Now see here, skipper," began the police sergeant, who was also close to losing his temper, "I didn't ask to come on this trip and, what's more, I intend to file some very serious complaints against you as soon as we're back in harbour!" Then, to add weight to his words, he fished his notebook and pencil out of his tunic pocket. "In fact, if you'd start by giving me your full name and address, I'll take a few details now—"

At that precise moment everything seemed to happen at once. There was a loud grinding and grating sound from the bottom of the boat. At the same time, the fishing-boat's prow rose sharply and steeply. The three men lost their footing and tumbled to the deck where they disappeared, temporarily, beneath the wet and slippery catch. The wicker baskets slid across the deck, rattled against the bulwarks and bounced over the side.

Hugo McMurdo, sprightly despite his advancing years, was

the first to emerge, gasping, from underneath the pile of fish, followed sheepishly by the other two. All three of them grabbed at whatever was handy for support and gazed around.

The *Highland Lassie* was leaning over dangerously, her mast tilted at a crazy angle to the horizon. The catch shifted, slowly, and slid over the starboard bow.

A tell-tale gushing sound came from the hold.

"Ah fear we've struck a rock the noo!" cried the old Scot. "And ah've an awfu' feelin' the wee boat's done for, dy'ken!"

"Beg pardon, skipper?" said the bosun. "I didn't quite catch what you said?"

Hugo McMurdo's weatherbeaten face turned almost purple as he seethed in silent anger and shook a gnarled fist at the cloudless sky.

Leaving the Inflatable Shop behind them, Samuel Swain and Henry Hollins set off across the white sand towards the ridge of jagged rocks.

When they had completed overhauling their craft, it had been decided that the two of them would go out and explore the surrounding area while Augusta and Mildred Pryce remained behind to take care of the shop.

The sun had come out, suddenly, and there was not a trace of wind. Henry wondered at the silence of the afternoon. He wondered too at the absence of any trees or grass or, indeed, of anything *growing* on the island—if island it was. For they still had no idea where they were. Augusta's suggestion that they might have been blown out into space and drifted onto another planet was quite ridiculous . . . All the same, they did seem to have landed in rather a curious place.

Just to be on the safe side, Henry fell in step and walked a little closer to the captain.

As the man and the boy approached the rock behind which he was standing, the tallest of the alien creatures tightened his grip on his laser-pistol. Then, when the newcomers were no more than a couple of metres away, the alien stepped out.

Henry and Samuel pulled up short. Their mouths fell open in surprise at the sight of the three-eyed green figure that confronted them. Their first instinct was to run, but flight seemed hopeless. Their fears increased as the tall alien was joined by another, then another—then a whole crowd of similarly armed three-eyed green-skinned creatures.

The tallest of the aliens took a step towards them. His silver space-suit glistened in the sunlight. The antennae quivered, excitedly, on top of his head.

"I say," said the alien space-creature, his three eyes blinking with delight. "What an absolutely *splendid* surprise! We weren't expecting visitors, were we, chaps?"

The other alien space-creatures shook their heads and murmured their agreement.

"We've been stuck on this island for weeks and weeks," continued their leader. "We're *positively* sick of the sight of each other. Isn't that so, chaps?"

The green-faced aliens nodded, enthusiastically, and their antennae wobbled about so much it seemed as if they might drop off.

"Too true," said one of their number.

"You wouldn't chuckle," said another.

"We've been bored out of our tiny skulls," said a third.

Samuel was the first to recover his composure. He stepped forward, holding out his hand to the tallest of the aliens. "I'm Samuel Swain," he announced. "An' the young 'un 'ere is 'enry 'ollins."

"Pleased to meet you both," replied the alien. "My name's Nigel Peters. But, if it's all the same to you, I won't shake hands—some of this green stuff might come off and then I'd get a fearful ear-bashing."

"Isn't it real then?" asked Henry.

Before the tall alien could reply, a round short red-faced man puffed into view around the rock, panting after his climb up the rise. "*Dònner und Blitzen*, Nigel!" said the new arrival. "You vill get more than der bashing of der ear, if you go vandering off vun more time!"

"Sorry, Mr von Himmelshraft," said the tallest alien, hanging his head in shame and kicking at the sand with a silver space-boot. "We just got fed up of hanging around. It won't happen again."

The short round man, who was wearing a safari jacket, jodhpurs, shiny brown riding-boots, and a monocle in one eye, and had a photographer's view-finder hanging round his neck, struck his forehead with the heel of his palm. "Ach!" he snorted. "*You* are gettink fed up? *I* am gettink fed up! Der cameraman is gettink fed up! Der *wardrobe peoples* is gettink fed up! Even der *clapper-boy* is gettink fed up! But ve vill not leave until der picture is finished! I, Oscar von Himmelshraft, am tellink you so! You vill all report at vonce to der make-up fraulein and haf more of der green make-up put on your bodies.

Do you hear?"

The alien creatures groaned their assent.

Mr von Himmelshraft stooped and picked up the eye which had fallen off the tallest alien's forehead into the sand. "Here, Nigel," said von Himmelshraft, handing the alien his eye back. "Give this also to der make-up fraulein—ask her to fix it again but viz more sticky."

The tallest alien nodded and turned, sheepishly, to Henry and Samuel. "I'm afraid we've got to go now," he said. "I hope I see you again."

"Same here," said Henry.

The tall alien turned and led his fellow alien creatures back between the rocks, the way they had come.

Mr von Himmelshraft clicked the heels of his shiny brown riding-boots together as he turned to Henry and Samuel. "*Guten Tag!*" he said. "Allow me to introduce myself. I am Heinrich von Himmelshraft, der famous film director. I am making *Aliens from Outer Space*—der greatest film of my career."

"Swamp me!" said Samuel. "I sees it now—them weren't real space-creatures at all! They were on'y actors dressed up!"

"And we're not on a strange planet, after all!" said Henry. "We're still on earth!"

"Space-creatures? Strange planets?" The famous film director threw back his head and laughed. "*Nein, nein*—ve are on der small island not far from der famous England seaside town—how do you say it?—*Cockleton-on-der-Ocean. Ja*?"

"Home!" smiled Henry, turning to Samuel. "Then we *were* rowing in the right direction after all."

"That we were, young 'un. Not that I ever 'ad any doubts, speakin' personally. I 'as a natural instinct about such things."

Heinrich von Himmelshraft frowned. "Sometimes I vish ve vere on der strange planet," he said. "I haf tried to make it *look* like der strange planet."

Henry glanced down at the pure white sand which, he now realized, was not real. "It *does* look like an alien planet, Mr von Himmelshraft," he said. "It fooled me."

The famous film director pulled himself up to his full height, proudly. He came almost to Samuel's shoulder. "Ven Heinrich von Himmelshraft makes der film every last detail is correct. *Ja?* Over der hill I haf had constructed der most vonderful interplanetary space-craft out of der plastic und der cardboard."

"Great!" said Henry. "Can we see it?"

"Vy not?" said Heinrich von Himmelshraft, sadly. "Perhaps you vill be der only peoples that do—it vill never be seen on der cinema-screens."

"Why's that then, shipmate?" asked Samuel. "What's wrong?"

"Der dreadful veather!" growled the famous film director. "Six veeks ve haf been here and every day—rain, rain, und more rain! It vashes der green stuff off der aliens' faces. It makes der cardboard interplanetary space-craft soggy." Mr von Himmelshraft sighed.

"It isn't raining now," said Henry.

"*Nein* . . ." said the famous film director. He frowned, rubbed his hand across the top of his bald head, and pointed across at the Inflatable Shop. "Vat is dat?" he said.

"Why, cully," said Samuel, "that there's our craft—an' I'm 'er captain."

"Actually, it isn't really a ship at all," said Henry. "It's a shop—we flew here in it."

"You *flew*?" The famous film director's eyes opened wide and he made flapping movements with his arms. "In a *shop*?"

Henry nodded, vigorously. "We didn't mean to fly. It was an accident really. We just . . . took off. But once we started it was quite easy. The shop's got gas-inflated boats and swimming-rings and things all round the sides."

"Vunderbar!" said Mr von Himmelshraft, clasping his hands together in delight.

"Would you like to see over her, shipmate?" asked Samuel.

"I must!" cried the famous film director. "I haf just had a brilliant idea for der scene for der new film!"

And, without waiting for Samuel and Henry, he set off with short quick strides, across the beach towards the Inflatable Shop.

8

A man with a brown moustache, wearing a blue suit and a black bowler hat, was measuring the empty space on the promenade where the Inflatable Shop had previously stood.

The area had been roped off, temporarily, in order that the general public would not disturb him. A handful of holiday-makers, with nothing better to do, were watching from behind the rope.

Detective Sergeant Roland Rakesby of New Scotland Yard rolled up his tape measure and entered his findings in his notebook.

"Excuse me! I say!"

The detective sergeant pretended that he hadn't heard the woman who was calling across to him. He stooped, picked up a piece of well-sucked seaside rock and studied it through his magnifying glass. A lot of the lettering had gone but he could still read: ". . . *kleton-on-Sea.*" Rakesby popped the rock in a plastic-bag which bore a label marked "Exhibit A".

"You in the bowler-hat! I'm talking to you!" persisted Emily Hollins.

"I don't think he's heard you," said Albert, who was standing next to his wife.

"Of course he's heard me!" snapped Emily. "He's ignoring me, that's what!"

The nearby watchers murmured their agreement.

The detective sergeant sucked in his cheeks and blew out his breath, making a whistling noise through his moustache. He could do without this kind of interference, he thought.

It was purely by chance that Rakesby was on the case. He had been holidaying in Cockleton-on-Sea with his wife, Marjory, and the twins, Greta and Greville. That morning, while helping the children to build a sandcastle, Mrs Rakesby had lost her wedding ring in the sand.

The detective sergeant had called in at the local police station to report the loss. First of all, he had met a young constable who had been extremely helpful. *Hooper*, was it? Or *Hepper*? Something like that. And then that superintendent chap had stuck his nose in. What was *he* called? Amplewood or Rumpleforth or something. Anyway, the fact had emerged that Rakesby was a New Scotland Yard detective and, before you could say "Elementary, my dear Watson", he had found himself transferred to this disappearing shop case.

"Some holiday!" muttered Rakesby to himself, as he strode across to where the nosey-parker woman was standing. "Were you addressing me, ma'am?" he said.

"I sincerely hope so," retorted Emily, not liking the detective's attitude. "I can't see anybody else with a bowler-hat on."

Several of the bystanders giggled and a fat lady carrying a bulging beach-bag laughed out loud.

"Perhaps I can be of assistance," said a voice.

The detective sergeant turned to find himself looking into the face of Police Superintendent Ampleforth. The police officer was dressed in civilian clothing and was carrying a round package under his arm.

"It's all right, Sergeant," began the superintendent, "I happen to know this lady—you carry on with the good work."

"Very good, sir!" said Rakesby, moving away. He had just spotted an ice-lolly stick which he had decided ought to be "Exhibit B".

The superintendent turned to Emily Hollins with a sympathetic smile. "You're only torturing yourself, you know. I do assure you, we're doing everything in our power to find your son." He pointed across at Rakesby. "That man is one of our top detectives—he's from New Scotland Yard."

"I hadn't realized that," said Emily.

"You need to be taken out of yourself," said the superintendent. "There's a very good film on at the Cinecentre. And there's the Crazy Golf. Or you could even stroll down as far as the Amusement Park and have a ride on the Wild Mouse. I often do that myself when I'm feeling a bit down in the dumps."

"Why don't we, Emily?" coaxed Albert. "Do one of those things?"

Emily forced a brave smile and allowed her husband to lead her off along the promenade.

"Sergeant!" called the superintendent.

"Sir?" called back the detective.

"I just thought you might like to know that Constable Hopper has taken his spade and sieve onto the beach and is looking for your wife's wedding ring."

"Thank you, sir."

"He has a phenomenally high success record."

"Thank you very much indeed, sir."

"That's all, Sergeant—carry on."

"Sir!"

Detective Sergeant Rakesby's eagle eyes swept the ground for "Exhibit C".

Superintendent Ampleforth complimented himself as he moved away on his efficiency in deploying his small but capable force.

He had two excellent men, Sergeants Threadgold and Rakesby, investigating the Mysterious Case of the Disappearing Shop. He had young Hopper sieving the sand in Operation Wedding Ring. It certainly was a matter of "All Systems Go!" at Cockleton-on-Sea police station.

He was allowing himself the luxury of an afternoon off. The package he carried contained a magnificent red cabbage. There was an All-comers Vegetable Show that afternoon in the nearby village of Gunnersby Cove.

The superintendent smiled to himself. The good thing about it was that as long as young Hopper stayed on his knees, on the sand, sieve in hand, he presented no threat in the Vegetable Show's red cabbage section!

Ampleforth looked both ways and then sprinted across the promenade towards his parked car.

Further along the promenade, Emily and Albert Hollins had stopped outside the Cinecentre and were intently examining the poster:

Showing Today

HEINRICH VON HIMMELSHRAFT'S

masterpiece

THE PYRAMIDS OF DEATH

"I don't fancy that at all," sniffed Emily.

"The superintendent said it was very good," said Albert. "He's the chief-of-police round here—he must know what he's talking about."

Emily shook her head. "I'm sorry, Albert, *no.* I've seen Heinrich von What's-his-name's films before. I don't understand them—they're too far-fetched."

"How about the Crazy Golf then?"

Emily pulled a face.

"Or the Wild Mouse in the Amusement Park?"

Emily wrinkled her nose, disdainfully.

"I'll tell you what," said Albert, excitedly. He had just remembered something. "There's a Design-Yourself-A-Funny-Hat competition on the South Pier this afternoon."

"That sounds more like it," said Emily, taking her husband's arm. "What are we waiting for?"

The famous film director placed his soup spoon in his empty plate. "*Danke, Fräulein,*" he said. "You are most kind."

Mildred Pryce simpered like a schoolgirl and fiddled with her beads. "Not at all, Mr von Himmelshraft," she said, skittishly. "It was a pleasure. It isn't every day we get a famous film director dropping in for a meal!"

"I'm not surprised," scoffed Augusta, "if all you can offer them is a bowl of tinned lukewarm Oxtail soup."

"Have you made your mind up yet, Mr von Himmelshraft, about the new scene for your film?" Henry put in, quickly, before the Pryce sisters could continue the argument.

Heinrich von Himmelshraft rose, put his hand to his forehead and closed his eyes. The famous film director was thinking very hard. The captain and crew of the Inflatable Shop sat silent and still in order not to disturb the processes of the great man's mind. At last, Mr von Himmelshraft opened his eyes and smiled at the four travellers, benevolently.

"Mein friends," began the famous film director, "you vill all be pleased und honoured to know that I, Heinrich von Himmelshraft, haf decided to include your vunderful flyink shop in my new film."

"Great!" Henry Hollins' mouth dropped open.

Samuel Swain beamed, broadly, and exuded pride.

The Pryce sisters forgot their differences and smiled at each other, pleased as Punch.

"I haf der whole scene up here," said the famous film director, tapping his forehead.

The four travellers nodded, held their breath, and waited for the great man to continue.

"An interplanetary space-craft lands," began the famous film director, picking up the empty Oxtail soup-tin and bringing it down, gently, onto the table. "Out of der space-craft comes der horde of alien creatures. Dey are green all over und—*mein Gott*, vat is dis?—each vun of them has got three eyes! Dey have captured der strange empty planet, or so dey think. *Ja?* But, *nein*—not so! Here is a curious flyink shop!" And the famous film director used a sauce bottle to illustrate the Inflatable Shop. "So! Der alien space-creatures vish to capture der shop and der four peoples inside it."

"Are we going to be in the film then, Mr von Himmelshraft?" asked Henry.

The famous film director nodded, solemnly, and the captain and crew of the Inflatable Shop exchanged delighted glances.

"But vile der alien creatures are running down der beach, shooting off der laser-pistols—*Zap! Zap! Zap!*—der flyink shop will rise slowly . . . so . . ." And he demonstrated again with the empty soup tin. "Und so . . . Und away it goes—Up! Up! und avay—to distant vorlds beyond. Der End."

"Bravo," murmured Augusta.

"Bravo," whispered Mildred.

"Danke schön," said the famous film director, modestly.

"When are ye reckonin' on filmin' this then, shipmate?" asked Samuel.

Heinrich von Himmelshraft shrugged. "At vonce, of course—ven else? Vile der sun is shinink. How long vill it take to put der gas into der inflatables—so dat der shop is ready for leavink der ground?"

"Thirty minutes at the most, shipmate."

"Vunderbar!" cried the famous film director. "Then in thirty minutes ve vill shoot der scene!"

And, in thirty minutes exactly, the scene was set.

Fifty fearsome three-eyed space-creatures crouched in the shadow of the ridge of rocks. Their silver uniforms glinted in the sunlight; their antennae trembled in the slight breeze. They gripped their laser-guns and chattered, nervously, as the make-up lady moved along their line, carrying out last-minute repairs with a jar of green make-up and a pot of glue.

The Inflatable Shop, with Henry, Samuel, Augusta and Mildred on the veranda, was hovering about half a metre above the beach, at the water's edge, and needing just a touch of gas in one last large inflatable to send it rising into the sky.

Across the beach, megaphone in hand, Heinrich von Himmelshraft sat in a canvas chair which had his name printed in large black letters across the back. The camera-crews were poised and ready to record the scene. The clapper-boy waited, anxiously, clapper-board in hand.

There were a few tense, final seconds while they waited for the sun to slip out from behind a cloud.

"Stand by!" called the assistant director.

"Ready when you are, Mr von Himmelshraft!" called the sound recordist.

The famous film director chewed on his cigar and nodded.

"Quiet, please!" called the first assistant.

The line of alien creatures by the rock ridge fell silent. Nigel Peters, who had the important role of leader of the aliens, gripped his laser-gun and held his breath.

The famous film director threw his cigar-stub into the sand. "Roll 'em!" he shouted.

The cameras turned.

The clapper-boy held up his clapper-board and closed it, sharply. "Scene ninety-three," he called. "Take one!"

"Action!" shouted the famous film director through his megaphone.

Nigel Peters jumped to his feet and started off down the pure white sand, brandishing his laser-gun. "Eenie-meenie-itoo-aku-baku!" he cried, calling out the line of alien dialogue he had spent weeks memorizing from his script.

"Eenie-meenie-itoo-aku-baku!" echoed his fellow alien creatures, following their leader down the beach.

Heinrich von Himmelshraft nodded, approvingly, as the band of aliens pounded across the sand towards where the Inflatable Shop was hovering at the edge of the sea.

"Eenie-meenie-oolu!" shouted Nigel Peters, aiming his laser-pistol.

"Eenie-meenie-oolu!" shouted the following aliens, imitating their leader's words and actions.

On the veranda of the Inflatable Shop, Samuel Swain held the nozzle of the gas-tube at the ready. Henry Hollins stood at his captain's side, ready to switch on the inflating gas as soon as he was given his cue.

"Goodness!" gasped Mildred, as the green-skinned three-eyed aliens rushed towards them. "Don't they look *real*!"

"What rubbish!" snapped Augusta. "It's quite obvious they're only actors. I can see one of them wearing a wrist-watch! And that one there's even forgotten to take off his *socks*!"

All the same, Mildred was right. To anyone not in the know, the approaching horde of alien creatures *did* present a frightening sight. They more than satisfied the famous film director who was leaning forward in his chair, excitedly. "Vunderbar!" he murmured to himself.

Zap! Zap! Zap! went Nigel Peters' laser-pistol at a signal from the first assistant.

Zap-zap-zap-zap-zap-zap-zap-zap! went the lasers of the other aliens, and: *Pee-ang!* and *Pee-oww!* Red, green and orange laser beams flashed across the beach.

Then, when the leading alien was no more than twenty metres or so from the veranda—and Mildred Pryce later declared that she could see all three of the whites of Nigel Peters' eyes—Samuel Swain's arm swept down, giving Henry the signal he was waiting for.

"Now!" called Samuel.

Henry turned on the inflating gas.

Immediately, the Inflatable Shop began to rise—up, up and away—leaving the horde of alien creatures staring, helplessly, on the sand.

"Eenie-meenie-minie-maku!" shouted Nigel Peters, waving his fist.

"Eenie-meeni-minie-maku!" chanted the other aliens, brandishing their weapons.

But the Inflatable Shop was already growing smaller as it floated gently out to sea.

"I do hope Mr von Himmelshraft is satisfied with the scene," said Mildred.

"He can take or leave it," observed Augusta, primly. "I, for one, am not acting it again!"

Back on the beach, the famous film director was delighted. "Cut!" he called, and the cameras stopped turning. "How was it for you?" he shouted to his first cameraman.

"Okay for me, Mr von Himmelshraft."

"Okay for me too," called the sound-recordist.

"Vunderbar!" cried the famous film director, taking out another big cigar. "Print it!" he said.

Back on the veranda of the Inflatable Shop, the crew relaxed.

"We'd better turn round and go back now," said Augusta. "Before the island's out of sight."

Samuel Swain shuffled his feet and looked down at the planking. "Well, now, ma'am," he said. "That's easier said than done."

"Are you saying that you *can't* turn the shop round?" demanded Augusta.

"Wouldn't advise it, ma'am," said Samuel. He licked a forefinger and held it up. "Not in this weather—there's a freshening wind getting up again."

"But we didn't load up with any provisions! Or fresh water!"

"Unfortunately not, ma'am."

"Can't we put down the dinghy and row ourselves back?" asked Mildred. "The same way we got there in the first place."

The captain glanced down over the veranda. The wind *was* getting up again. Already, the sea's surface was white-flecked and heaving. Samuel shook his head. "I wouldn't care to take 'er down at all, ma'am. Matter o' fack, it'd be far wiser to take 'er up a piece or two until the wind's blown itself out."

"You stupid man!" snapped Augusta. "We're worse off now than ever before! And all for the sake of showing off in a film!"

"*You* didn't say anything at the time, Augusta," said Mildred. "You were just as pleased as any of us to be appearing in the picture."

"Fiddlesticks! You were the one who was primping and preening and making eyes at that ridiculous director!"

"I did not make eyes at him!"

"You gave him *soup*! That's worse than making eyes!"

"Ladies, ladies!" said Samuel Swain.

"*Sssshh!*" said Henry. "Do be quiet! I thought I heard someone shouting for help."

They peered back in the direction from which they had come—but the island was well out of sight.

"Ain't nobody about, young 'un," said Samuel. "Must 'ave bin your imagination."

"Help . . . *Help!*" This time there was no mistaking the cry that was carried on the wind. All four of them heard it plainly.

"Swamp me, you're right!" said Samuel. "On'y it seems to be comin' from up ahead o' us somewheres."

The four travellers moved round the veranda and scanned the foam-flecked sea.

"Over there!" cried Mildred, pointing to where a tiny lifeboat rose and fell, dangerously, in the heavy swell.

They could just make out the figures of three men in the boat. One was standing up, waving a red spotted handkerchief. The other two men were sitting down, facing each other.

Police Sergeant Edgar Threadgold, one of the seated men, was holding his helmet between his knees for safety's sake. Hugo McMurdo, the second seated figure, was clutching tight to a sacking-wrapped package that contained the few precious possessions he had managed to salvage from the wreck of the *Highland Lassie*.

"Ahoy there! Shop ahoy!" cried Bosun Throstlethwaite, frantically waving his spotted handkerchief.

"Och, mon, awa' wi' ye!" grumbled Hugo McMurdo. "It's

nae '*shop* ahoy!' ye're supposed to shout on sich occasions. It's '*ship* ahoy!' "

"But it *is* a shop, skipper," said the bosun. "You can see it's a shop as clear as day. It's coming straight towards us."

"Ah've nivver heard tell o' anything sae daft in a' mah born days!" muttered McMurdo, looking up. "Ah'll nae be saved by a travelling retail shop—ah'll be the laughin' stock o' Scotland. Ah'd rather drown."

A sudden thought occurred to the police sergeant. He remembered the words that were written on the scrap of paper he still carried in his pocket: *This is to let you know that I am somewhere over the sea in Samuel Swain's shop*. Could it be, he wondered, that he was at last coming to the end of his investigations? There couldn't be all that many shops knocking about the oceans.

"Wave to them again," said the police sergeant.

"There's no need," replied the bosun. "I think they've seen us."

Back on the veranda of the Inflatable Shop, Samuel turned to Henry. "If you nips inside an' feels at the back o' the fourth shelf down in the store-cupboard, young 'un, you'll find a rope-ladder. Fetch it 'ere to me—quick."

"Aye-aye, cap'n."

"Stand by to take on boarders!" cried Samuel, turning to the Pryce sisters. " 'As we anythin' left in the way o' soup?"

Mildred nodded. "A large tin of Mixed Vegetable and a small Minestrone," she announced.

"In which circumstance, ma'am, you'd best break open the larger o' the two. I reckons them poor souls will be in dire need o' sustenance once we gets 'em aboard."

"Aye-aye, captain!" Mildred followed Henry into the shop.

Augusta frowned. "I do hope you realize that all we'll have left will be one small tin of Minestrone?" she said.

"Yes, ma'am—and what o' that?"

"In the first place, I don't *like* Minestrone," snapped Augusta. "And in the second place, from now on, we'll have seven mouths to feed."

Samuel gazed at Augusta for several seconds, severely. "Ma'am, there is such a thing as a Code o' Manners when it comes to rescuin' shipwrecked mariners," he said, and added: "One doesn't stop to count the cost."

Augusta Pryce felt like biting off her tongue—she knew that Samuel was right.

"Here you are, captain," said Henry, returning with the rolled-up rope-ladder.

"Well done, shipmate."

Henry and the captain lashed the rope-ladder securely to the veranda rail and let the rungs down over the side. The bottom of the rope-ladder trailed at sea-level.

"Stand by, lifeboat!" yelled Samuel, as the Inflatable Shop drifted over the shipwrecked men.

In the pitching sea below, the police sergeant kept a tight grip around the bosun's legs as Throstlethwaite stood upright in the heaving lifeboat and made a grab for the rope-ladder. He managed to get hold of it at his second attempt.

The police sergeant snatched up a length of ship's rope in order to lash the bottom of the rope-ladder to the lifeboat's stern. Then all that stood between the three men and safety was the relatively simple task of scrambling up the ladder.

The bosun was the first to step onto the veranda, followed closely by the police sergeant. McMurdo came last, clutching his sacking-parcel under one arm and grumbling to himself.

"Welcome aboard, shipmates," said Samuel, "an' right glad we are to 'ave bin of service."

The bosun and the police sergeant mumbled their thanks at being rescued from the raging deep, but the old Scot could manage no more than a scowl.

"Who's in charge o' this flyin' hen-hoose?" he growled.

"I am—Samuel Swain, sir, at your service!"

"Och, call yoursel' the captain, do ye?" grunted McMurdo. "Then no doot ye'll be guid enough to tell me where we're headin' for the noo?"

Samuel looked down at the planking in some embarrassment. He was forced to admit that he did not know.

"Ye dinna *know*! An' ye ca' yoursel' a captain?" McMurdo's voice was scornful.

"It isn't Mr Swain's fault that he's no idea where we're headed," said Henry, loyally leaping to his captain's defence. "For one thing, we've no charts or compass."

"Nae charts an' nae compass?" grumbled the grizzled Scot in disbelief. "Mon, some skippers would go tae sea wi'oot their heads if they didnae hae them screwed on!" He thrust his sacking-wrapped package into Samuel's hands. "Ye'd better hae these then, laddie," he continued, "for inside there is the charts an' compass off ma' own wee boat, God rest her."

Samuel accepted the package, gratefully. "That's all I need to chart a course," he said, leading them inside.

"Ah'm on'y givin' ye the lend o' them mind," said Hugo McMurdo. "Ah shall need them back as soon as we get to port."

Samuel set to work at once, studying the charts.

Mildred Pryce looked up at their guests. "Soup is served," she said.

"What kind of soup is it?" asked the bosun.

"Mixed Vegetable."

"My favourite!" said the bosun.

"Women-folk in the galley, is it?" grumbled the Scots skipper. "Why, mon, ah'd nae hae a lassie doin' the cookin' aboard any craft o' mine!" But, all the same, he sniffed appreciatively at the aroma that met him.

Threadgold turned to Henry. "You must be Henry Hollins?" he said.

"However did you know that?"

The police sergeant felt inside his pocket and took out the crumpled note. "I have reason to believe," he said, "that you posted this note in a bottle?"

Henry's face lit up. His message *had* been found after all.

"Your mum and dad, young man," said the police sergeant, "are worried stiff about you."

Samuel Swain turned towards them, compass in one hand and chart in the other. "If my calculations are correct," he chuckled, "this wind is carrying us straight for Cockleton-on-Sea—we'll be home by five o'clock this evening!"

9

Although the Inflatable Shop had set out on its flight unnoticed by the townspeople and holiday-makers, the same could not be said of its return.

And even before the flying shop was first sighted, by a lone lady angler fishing off the end of the pier, the entire town was talking of nothing but the strange events of the past two days.

The entire front page of the evening's edition of the *Cockleton-on-Sea Telegraph and Argus* was given over to the latest details of the story. Right across the top of the page, in enormous capital letters, was the headline:

VANISHING SHOP—LATEST NEWS!

And underneath, it said, in only slightly smaller lettering:

NEW SCOTLAND YARD CALLED IN!

And now, as well as the pictures of the vacant space on the promenade and Police Sergeant Threadgold, which had appeared in the earlier editions, there was a third photograph depicting Detective Sergeant Roland Rakesby, holding up a small plastic bag labelled "Exhibit J". The bag, although it didn't reveal it in the newspaper story, contained a Smoky-

Bacon-Flavour Potato Crisp packet.

When the lady angler threw down her rod and ran back along the pier, crying: "It's coming back! It's in the sky! It's *here*!" not surprisingly everybody knew what she was shouting about.

The news spread like wildfire.

Crowds thronged the promenade rail.

The amusement-arcades and sea-front gift-shops emptied as if by magic.

Along the sea-front hotels, the Buona Vista, the St Claire, the Fredna, the Albemarle, Clovellies, the New Waterloo and the Sea View, the bedroom windows were flung open and eager, excited faces peered up into the sky.

Business along the pier was halted as hundreds of holiday-makers jostled to get a good view of the Inflatable Shop's return. Traffic along the promenade was brought to a standstill. Police Superintendent Ampleforth, driving back triumphantly from the Gunnersby Cove Vegetable Show and proud possessor of the Red Rosette award for the best red cabbage, found himself caught up in a mile-long traffic jam.

Every face in Cockleton-on-Sea was turned upwards, gazing out to sea. Every face, that is, except for one: Constable Hopper, on his hands and knees, toiled tirelessly with sieve and spade for lost wedding rings.

Up in the sky, on the veranda of the Inflatable Shop, Samuel Swain, Henry Hollins, Augusta and Mildred Pryce, Hugo McMurdo, Frank Throstlethwaite and Edgar Threadgold all peered down across the sea at the approaching town.

"Well, young 'un," said Samuel, softly, "I reckons it's almost over."

"Are you sad that it's ending, Mr Swain?" asked Henry, who thought that he had detected a note of regret in the old sailor's voice.

"Aye," admitted Samuel with a sigh. "I reckons a life ashore is goin' to seem a mite dull arter all that's 'appened these last couple o' days."

"It'll be awfi' dull for me tae, mon," muttered Hugo McMurdo. "There'll be nae more trips to sea for me naether, now mah wee boatie's sunk the noo."

"It won't seem dull to me," announced Police Sergeant Threadgold. "I shall be glad to get my feet up on my office desk again! If there's one thing I've learned from this adventure, it's that there's worse things than the peace and quiet of Cockleton-on-Sea."

"It's taught me a lesson too," said Augusta, quietly. "I'm going to stop quarrelling with Mildred in future. Goodness, if *sisters* can't get on together, what hope is there for the rest of the *world*?"

Mildred smiled at Augusta, and nodded her agreement.

"I've had enough of seafaring," announced the bosun. "I've got a bit of cash stowed away. I reckon I'll buy myself a little business and settle down to a restful life ashore."

Samuel Swain scratched at the stubble on his chin, tugged at his ear-ring and studied the bosun. "I don't suppose, shipmate," he said at last, "as 'ow you'd care to consider taking this place off my hands?"

"You're not serious?" said the bosun, gazing round the shop in delight—it was just the sort of small shop he had in mind.

"As serious as I ever was in all my life, shipmate."

"But why would you want to sell a place like this?"

"I've already said, cully," explained Samuel. "These last couple o' days 'ave given me a 'ankerin' to get back to sea. If you c'n give me a fair price for the old shop, I knows where there's a right handy little fishin'-smack goin' cheap. I c'd just fancy a spot o' fishin' up and down the coast."

"An' a canny hash y'd mak' o' that, mon!" hooted Hugo McMurdo. "Fishin', is it? Why, ye've nae more idea o' findin' y'r way aroond these waters, laddie, than a sporran in a spin-drier!"

"'Appen so," said Samuel, with a smile, "an' on the other 'and, 'appen not—an' 'appen I shall take someone along wi' me—someone as c'n lay 'old of a few charts an' a compass an' suchlike."

"Y'r nae meanin' me, mon?" gasped the old Scot.

"If you've a mind to accompany me," said Samuel.

"Ah'm no easy mon to get alang wi' the noo," admitted McMurdo. "Ah'm known as a cranky old divvil, d'y'ken?"

"Aye, shipmate," said Samuel. "I ken that fine—but I reckons between us we might 'it it off."

"Hoots, mon," cackled the old Scot, gleefully, "ye've got yoursel' a partner, mon!" And turning to the bosun he went on: "Did ye hear that, bosun? Ah've found a braw laddie at last that speaks the same lingo as mahsel!"

"What was that, skipper?" replied the bosun. "I didn't quite catch what you said."

"Nivver mind," said McMurdo, "dinna fash yoursel'!"

"Look, everybody!" cried Henry, pointing down over the veranda. "Look down there!"

They were now cruising over the beach. The shop was flying so low that its occupants could make out the sand-castles and knots of seaweed. And they could also see the upturned faces of the townspeople and holiday-makers who jammed the promenade and pier.

"Great heaven," murmured Augusta. "Do you think they are there because of *us*?"

At that moment, a cry went up from a tall, thin man in Boy Scout uniform who had brought a party of Wolf Cubs on a day's outing to the seaside. "Three cheers for the flying shop!" he cried, as its shadow sailed across him. Then, taking off his scout-master's hat he waved it in the air. "Hip-hip—"

"Horray!" A piping cheer went up from the pack of Wolf Cubs.

The call was taken up by the crowd: "HIP-HIP-HOORAY!"

"Aye, ma'am," said Samuel, in answer to Augusta's question. "I reckons they are out there to welcome us back! I'll be a sea-cook's uncle! We must be famous. 'Old tight, shipmates—I'm goin' to set us down."

The passengers and crew of the Inflatable Shop took a firm grip on the veranda rail as Samuel set about decreasing height.

"*Tttttssssss* . . ." hissed the gas as it escaped through the open valves.

Slowly and steadily, the shop began its final descent.

It would have been a fairy-tale ending to the story if Samuel Swain had managed to bring his shop down at the exact point from which it had set off. But, alas, real life is rarely like a fairy story. Samuel contrived to set the shop down slap-bang in the centre of the South Pier.

"Hold back those crowds, men!" shouted Superintendent Ampleforth, who had had the good sense to abandon his car in the traffic-jam and had assembled his force in order to assist at the landing.

Detective Sergeant Rakesby and Constable Hopper linked arms and braced themselves against the mass of onlookers who were struggling to get a better view.

"I've got something for you, sergeant," said Hopper, trying to prevent his helmet from being pushed over his eyes as he held back the jostling crowd.

"Oh," said the detective sergeant. "And what's that?"

"Your wife's wedding ring. It's in my tunic-pocket. I found it on the sands. I'll give it to you later."

"Great!" said Rakesby. "Marjory will be pleased!"

Further conversation was not possible as the Inflatable Shop touched the pier's planking and the crowd surged forward.

"Stand back!" entreated the superintendent. "Give them room to disembark!"

One by one, the captain, crew and passengers stepped off the veranda and onto the pier: Samuel Swain, Augusta Pryce, Mildred Pryce, Sergeant Threadgold, Bosun Throstlethwaite, Hugo McMurdo and, last of all, Henry Hollins.

A woman, wearing a curious construction on her head, broke through the two-man police cordon, rushed across and swept Henry into her arms.

"Hello, Mum," said Henry. "What's that on your head?"

Emily Hollins put up her hands and lifted down the object which appeared to have been fashioned out of egg-boxes, yoghurt-cartons and silver-foil. "Silly me!" she laughed. "It's

my entry in the Make-Yourself-A-Funny-Hat competition. I'd quite forgotten I still had it on!" She hugged Henry yet again.

Samuel Swain waited until the touching reunion was over before taking his leave of Henry. "Goodbye, young 'un," he said, patting the boy on the shoulder.

"Goodbye, Mr Swain," said Henry. "I hope you manage to

buy your fishing-boat. If you do, can I come out for a trip with you next year?"

"It ain't a question o' *can* you, shipmate," chuckled Samuel. "I reckons as 'ow you'll *'ave* to. Swamp me, I couldn't 'ave coped these last two days if it 'adn't 'ave bin for you."

Henry smiled, proudly, and shook the old sailor by the hand.

When all of the leave-takings were over, Albert Hollins, his wife Emily, and their son Henry strolled back towards the Sea View Private Hotel.

"It strikes me," said Albert, who had been deep in thought for some time, "that that Samuel Swain isn't such a bad sort of chap, after all."

"He's *superb!*" said Henry.

"I'll say this," said Emily. "He seems to have taken good care of you on your travels—*and* you seem to have enjoyed yourself."

"I had a great time," said Henry. "I was in a film."

"That's nice," said Emily.

"What's been happening here?" asked Henry.

"Not a lot," said Albert, and then he was struck by a thought. "I'll tell you what you have missed though, that you'll kick yourself about."

"What's that?"

"Prawn cocktail starters. We had them for lunch."

"I don't mind particularly," said Henry. "It was worth giving that up for—what's on the menu for dinner tonight?"

"I don't know what we're having for a main course," said Emily, "but we're kicking off with Minestrone soup."

Henry pulled a face. "That won't please Augusta Pryce," he

said. "She hates Minestrone soup."

Later that evening, as the sun slid down behind the horizon, Frank Throstlethwaite wandered round the veranda of the Inflatable Shop. He had agreed a price with Samuel Swain and was now examining his purchase.

He reached up to touch a bobbing silver balloon which danced away from his outstretched hand, and looked around at the rest of his stock.

There were lifebelts in all shapes and sizes, multi-hued beach-balls, and swimming-rings fashioned like swans. There were inflated air-beds, one-child canoes, and two-adult dinghies. There were huge unsinkable green tortoises.

The inflated goods around the veranda stirred and swayed slightly in the late evening breeze.

"It looks to me," said Throstlethwaite to himself, "as if some of those goods could do with a touch of air."

He glanced around. There were two inflating machines, side by side, just inside the open door of the shop. Frank Throstlethwaite was puzzled. "Now, which one of those," he asked himself, "did Samuel say was air, and which one gas?"

The new proud proprietor of the Inflatable Shop shrugged. "There's only one way to find out," he told himself.

He picked up one of the lengths of plastic tube, applied the nozzle to the valve of a large dinghy, and switched on . . .

The Boy Who Sprouted Antlers

JOHN YEOMAN AND QUENTIN BLAKE

'As long as you set your mind on it and try hard enough, there's nothing you can't do,' said Miss Beddows to Billy when he declared that he simply couldn't make a basket. Billy liked the idea that he could do anything, but Melanie and Paul didn't agree.

'What about growing horns?' said Melanie. It was a challenge that Billy had to accept.

'Wildly improbable and cleverly sustained.' *Margery Fisher*

Hilarious reading for sevens and up.

My Best Fiend

SHEILA LAVELLE

'My best friend is called Angela Mitchell and she lives in the house next door.' There is nothing unusual about this opening description Charlie Ellis gives of her best friend, but the tales that follow reveal the very unusual scrapes these two friends seem to get into.

Pretty Angela's marvellous ideas usually lead to disaster. Like the time they got stuck on a single-track railway bridge over the River Thames with the rattle of train wheels getting closer and closer; and the time Angela accidentally caught an escaped circus lion in the back garden. But when Angela suggested burning down her dad's garage so that he could claim the insurance for a new one, Charlie really thought things had gone a bit too far. For somehow it's always plainer Charlie who ends up taking the blame, and the spelling mistake in her English essay really wasn't much of a mistake at all.